CAMBRIDGE SCHOOL CLASSICS PROJECT
CLASSICAL STUDIES

Book IV.
Athens: City and Empire

compiled from Thucydides, Plutarch and
other ancient sources by
ERNEST HEATLEY and
MARGARET WIDDESS

D1493025

CAMBRIDGE
UNIVERSITY PRESS

Published by the Press Syndicate of the University of Cambridge
The Pitt Building, Trumpington Street, Cambridge CB2 1RP
40 West 20th Street, New York, NY 10011-4211, USA
10 Stamford Road, Oakleigh, Melbourne 3166, Australia

This book, an outcome of work done for the Schools Council before its closure,
is published under the aegis of SCAA Enterprises Limited,
Newcombe House, 45 Notting Hill Gate, London W11 3JB

© SCAA Enterprises Limited 1989

First published 1989
Reprinted 1995

Printed in Malta by Interprint Limited

British Library cataloguing-in-publication data
Thucydides
   Athens: city and empire. – (Cambridge school
classics project. Classical studies 13–16; GK. 4)
   1. Athenian empire. Political events
   I. Title II. Plutarch III. Heatley, Ernest IV.
Widdess, Margaret
   938′.5

Library of Congress cataloguing-in-publication data
Athens, city and empire/compiled from Thucydides,
   Plutarch, and other ancient sources by Ernest
Heatley and Margaret Widdess. (Classical studies
13–16/Cambridge School Classics Project: bk. 4)
   1. Athens (Greece) – History.   I. Thucydides.
   II. Plutarch.   III. Heatley, Ernest.   IV. Widdess,
Margaret.   V. Series: Classical studies 13–16; bk. 4.
   DF28.A87   1989
   938′.5 – dc20

ISBN 0 521 38874 0   DS

Thanks are due to the following for permission to reproduce illustrations:
cover, p.64 Alison Frantz; pp.6 (left), 8, 72 (bottom), 73 (top), 74
The Trustees of the British Museum; pp.6 (right), 29, 52 Musée du Louvre,
Paris; pp.7, 44 Ashmolean Museum Oxford; pp.12, 21, 58 (bottom), 75
Museum of Classical Archaeology, Cambridge; p.13 Olympia Museum; pp.20,
62 (top), 63, 67, 68 American School of Classical Studies at Athens: Agora
Excavations; p.23 Lewis Collection, Corpus Christi College, Cambridge;
p.30 National Archaeological Museum, Athens; p.34, 55 Loyola University of
Chicago; p.37 Mansell Collection; p.49 British School at Athens;
p.51 Antikenmuseum Berlin, Staatliche Museum Preussischer Kulturbesitz;
p.57 (left) Prof. Elisha Linder, University of Haifa; p.57 (right) Acropolis
Museum, Athens; p.62 (bottom) Thames and Hudson; p.69 Athens
Epigraphic Museum p.70, 72 (top) J.J. Coulton from *Ancient Greek Architects
at Work*, published by Oxbow Books; p.71 Werner Forman Archive. Other
photographs by E. Heatley.

Maps by Reg Pigott.

Contents

Apart from ancient source material, the text consists of editorial and background material. This editorial material is distinguished by smaller type and marginal rules. In the 'Events and Personalities' section, references to the ancient sources are given in the left-hand margin – e.g. Thucydides I.89–90 means Thucydides *History of the Peloponnesian War* Book I, chapters 89–90. The book covers the middle years of the fifth century B.C. and dates are given in the right-hand margin.

Race and gender

Most of this book consists of new translations of ancient authors, so that students can judge for themselves the extent of any bias and prejudice which may have existed in the ancient world. Words such as 'he', 'man' and 'barbarian' are used as they were in the original Greek. In the editorial passages, however, 'he' denotes solely the masculine.

I The Background

I.1 Introduction

The photograph on the cover shows a view of Athens familiar to millions throughout the world. The buildings standing on the Acropolis hill have been admired and copied over the centuries. Yet less than fifty years before work on them began the whole of Athens, both city and Acropolis, had been totally devastated, its buildings ransacked and burned by an invading Persian army.

This book describes the events of those fifty years, focusing on two of the leading personalities of the time, Cimon and Pericles.

City states

The city of Athens lies in eastern Greece about 8 kms (5 miles) from the sea. Surrounding it is the region called Attica, which is about 80 kms (50 miles) from side to side at its widest point. By about 700 B.C. all the separate communities of Attica had come together under the leadership of Athens and the whole area considered itself a single state – or *polis*, as the Greeks called it.

Ancient Greece was made up of several dozen of these 'city states', each with its own laws and government. Five of the most important are shown on the map.

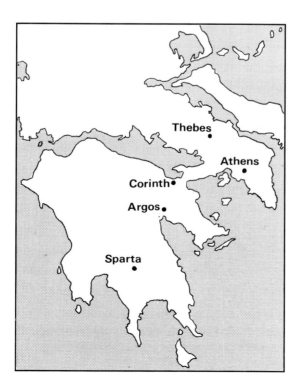

I.2 Attica: what were its resources?

As members of an independent state, the people of Attica had to be sure that they could feed and defend themselves. This meant making the best use of the resources available.

The produce of the land shows how extremely mild the climate is. Plants which cannot even grow in other countries, here produce fruit. The sea which surrounds the land is also highly productive. The seasonal produce given by the gods comes in here much earlier than elsewhere and continues for much longer.

Yet the land is not just excellent for seasonal things, which grow and die off each year; it also has good things which last for ever. There is a great abundance of stone, from which the most beautiful temples and altars are made, as well as fine-looking statues to the gods. Many Greeks and

The climate of Attica

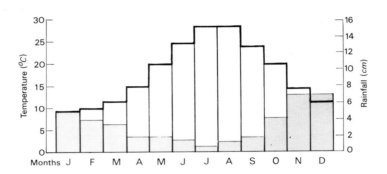

An Attic amphora made in the sixth century B.C.

Attic wine jug found in Italy. 5th–4th century B.C.

An Athenian tetradrachm. About 450 B.C.

foreigners need this stone. There is also silver beneath the ground which is clearly the gift of the gods. There are many states that border Attica, both by land and sea, but not one of them contains even the smallest vein of silver ore.

Xenophon *Resources* 1–3

The mountains of Athens are Pentelikon, where the quarries are, Parnes, which provides wild boars and bears for hunting, and Hymettos, which produces the best pasture for bees.

Pausanias *Guide Book to Greece* 1.32.1

You will be aware that we eat more imported corn than any other people, and we import more of it from the Black Sea than anywhere else.

Demosthenes *Speech against Leptines* 31

The land looks like the skeleton of a sick man. Only the bare bones are left; all the fat and soft earth have slipped away.

Plato *Critias* III B

Athens has the finest and safest accommodation for ships, where they can run into port and ride at anchor without fear even in bad weather. In most other cities merchants have to exchange one cargo for another, because they cannot use the local currency in other states. In Athens, too, they can take away in exchange all sorts of things that people need. But if they don't want to take away a return cargo they can do good business by taking silver, since they will always make a profit on it, wherever they sell it.

Xenophon *Resources* 3.2

Attica

I.3 Athens 600–500 B.C.

In 600 B.C. Athens was a smallish town and the government was in the hands of a few wealthy families. They held all the important positions and were in sole control of the law. Most of the citizens worked on the land and were extremely poor; many of them were in debt. For those who could not repay their debts there was only one solution – to sell themselves into slavery. As the situation grew worse, it seemed as if the result would be civil war.

594 B.C. Solon the lawgiver

Amidst violence, Solon was elected to try and settle the differences between rich and poor. Although he was not entirely successful, he did at least give the poor the guaranteed right to vote in the assembly of the people, to appeal to the court of the people and to serve on juries. He also helped the poor by passing a law which said that no one could be made a slave if he could not repay his debts.

Under Solon's system, the people were divided into four classes according to the wealth produced from their land. The poorest of all did not have to pay taxes, but they were not allowed to hold public office. Only the wealthiest of all could become one of the nine *archons* who ruled the city.

545 B.C. Peisistratos the tyrant

The Greek word *tyrannos* meant someone who seized power illegally. There were tyrants in several Greek cities, and not all of them were harsh rulers. Peisistratos, who seized power in Athens, was a patron of the arts and responsible for new

Peisistratos built the popular 'house of the nine fountains', in which a natural spring was made to run through nine lions' heads. This Athenian vase was made in about 520 B.C. and exported to Italy. The writing on the left says 'Fair flowing spring' – the name of the spring used by Peisistratos.

public buildings. He won the support of the peasant farmers, and gave them land taken from the rich.

After Peisistratos died in 527 B.C., one of his sons was murdered; the other son became a harsh and unpopular ruler before being driven out with the help of a Spartan army.

507 B.C. Cleisthenes the reformer

Cleisthenes was a leading opponent of the tyrants and became one of the archons in 507 B.C. He reorganised the Athenians into ten 'tribes' so that each consisted of people from different parts of Attica – some from the city, some from the coast and some from the countryside. Every year, 50 men from each tribe were chosen by lot to be members of the *Council of the Five Hundred*. The Council prepared business in advance for the *Assembly*, and then saw that the decisions of the Assembly were carried out.

However, Cleisthenes kept Solon's class system so that wealth was still the key to power in the city.

I.4 The Persian Wars

On the coast of Asia Minor (modern Turkey) was an area called Ionia. It was named after Greeks from the Ionian tribe who had settled there. Originally these people had been free, but gradually they had come under the rule of the vast Persian empire. In 496 B.C. the Athenians helped their fellow Ionian Greeks in an unsuccessful rebellion against the Persians, and this gave the Persian king an excuse for a war against Athens.

In 490 B.C. he sent an expedition by sea which landed at Marathon on the coast of Attica. The Athenians, helped by only a few of their neighbours, were hopelessly outnumbered. But their commander Miltiades tricked the Persians into charging through the centre of the Athenian army, only to find themselves surrounded by the troops on each wing. News of the victory was taken to Athens by a runner who was said to have collapsed and died after delivering his message. The modern 'marathon' race is run over 40.195 kms (26 miles 385 yards) – the distance between Athens and the battlefield at Marathon.

Ten years later in 480 B.C. the Persians returned. This time they came by both land and sea. In the north of Greece the Persians defeated the Greeks at Thermopylae, a battle made famous by the 300 Spartans who stayed to fight and face certain death, rather than retreat in the face of the enemy.

The Persians then moved south towards Athens, and the Athenians decided to evacuate their city and encamp on the island of Salamis. The city was ransacked, but this didn't stop the Greeks winning a sea battle in the narrow straits between Salamis and Attica. The victory was masterminded by the Athenian general Themistocles.

In the following year (479 B.C.) the Greeks finally drove the Persians out of their land, in a battle which took place near the town of Plataea, just outside the borders of Attica. This time it was a Spartan, Pausanias, who led the Greeks to victory.

The Greeks also won a second sea battle, at Mycale on the shores of Ionia. There was a tradition that it happened on exactly the same day as the battle of Plataea.

II After the Persian Wars

After their defeat, the Persians were pursued by the Greeks, who freed some of the cities on the coast of Ionia which had been under Persian rule. The Greeks then returned home.

II.1 Athens builds her walls

Thucydides
I.89–90

478 B.C.

Now that the enemy had left, the Athenians immediately began to bring back from hiding their children, their wives and any possessions they still had. They also began to rebuild their city walls. Only a few sections of their city wall were standing and most of their houses had collapsed, except for a few in which the Persian leaders had encamped.

When the Spartans realised what the Athenians were intending to do, they sent representatives to Athens. The Spartans themselves were not pleased to see Athens or any other city with fortifications, but it was their allies who were most anxious. They were frightened by the size of the Athenian fleet, which had not existed before, and by the boldness the Athenians had shown when they were fighting against the Persians. The Spartan representatives demanded that the Athenians should stop building their own fortifications. They also demanded that the Athenians should join forces with them and pull down all the fortifications still standing in cities outside the Peloponnese. The Spartans did not say what they were really getting at and why they were suspicious; instead, they made out that if the Persians came back, there would be no stronghold from which the enemy could launch an attack, if the Greek cities were unfortified. They said that the Peloponnese could serve

The North Wall of the Acropolis. The stone drums were originally intended for a temple to celebrate the victory at Marathon. When the Persians returned ten years later, they ransacked Athens and left the Acropolis devastated.

10

everyone, both as a place to retreat to and as a place to attack from.

After the Spartans had made this speech, the Athenians took Themistocles' advice and sent the Spartans away immediately, saying that they would themselves send representatives to discuss the matters that the Spartans had raised. Once they had gone, Themistocles told the Athenians to choose representatives to go to Sparta; he himself would go as soon as possible, but they should not send the others for the time being. He told them that instead they should wait until they had built their walls high enough to serve as defences; and they were to demolish any house or public building if it could be used in the building job. 'Leave everything at Sparta to me,' he said, and, with these instructions, he set off.

II.2 Themistocles in Sparta

Thucydides
I.90–1

When Themistocles arrived at Sparta, he did not go to the authorities there, but kept putting them off and making excuses. If anyone asked why he did not come before the assembly of the people, he replied that he was waiting for the other representatives. 'They have been held up in Athens', he explained. 'Some business cropped up that they had to deal with. They'll definitely be here soon, though; in fact I'm surprised that they are not here by now.'

The Spartans regarded Themistocles as a friend and so they believed him, but they felt they also had to take seriously the reports of other people who kept arriving from Athens. These people declared that fortifications were being built and that they were already quite high. Themistocles saw what was going on. 'Don't be put off by rumours,' he said. 'Why don't you send some of your own people, men you can really trust? They can have a look and when they get back they can tell you what's happening.' The Spartans did as he suggested. Themistocles then sent a secret message to the Athenians telling them to keep the Spartans in Athens in as friendly a way as possible and not to let them go until the Athenian representatives had returned from Sparta. This was because his fellow representatives had now arrived from Athens. They had told him that the fortifications were now high enough, and Themistocles was afraid that if the Spartans found this out from their own people, he and his fellow Athenians might not be allowed to return to Athens.

The Athenians detained the Spartans, as Themistocles had instructed. Themistocles then went to the Spartan assembly and at last spoke to them openly.

'People of Sparta', he said, 'Athens' city walls are now restored and the city is fortified well enough to protect our people. If you or your allies want to hold any discussions with us, by all means send representatives. But now you know that we are people who can judge for ourselves what our own interests are and what interests we have in common with the rest of Greece. I say that either no city should have walls, or our walls should be approved.'

11

The Spartans concealed their anger and grudgingly agreed with the Athenians. The representatives from both cities returned home.

Thucydides
I.93

This was how the Athenians came to acquire their city walls in such a short time. Even now it is obvious that they were built in a hurry. The foundations are of different kinds of stone which have not been properly worked; each stone is laid down just as it was brought. There are many pillars from tombs and bits of sculpture all built into the wall. The people built the walls beyond the old boundaries of the city and in their haste they left no source of building stone undisturbed.

Statue base, found in the walls built by Themistocles.

II.3   The Athenians secure their position

Thucydides
I.93

Themistocles also persuaded the Athenians to complete the walls of the port of Piraeus. (These had been begun earlier on his advice when he was archon.) He thought that Piraeus had an attractive position, with its three natural harbours, and that becoming a sea-faring people would help the Athenians to gain power. In fact, he was the first to speak out and say that they should rely on the sea. In so doing, he at once began to play his part in establishing the empire. He paid particular attention to the navy, as he apparently realised that it was easier for an expedition sent by the Persian king to reach Athens by sea rather than by land. He also considered that Piraeus was more useful than the city above and frequently insisted that if the Athenians were ever hard pressed on land, their best option would be to go down to Piraeus and resist all enemy attacks with their ships.

III Early life and career of Cimon

III.1 Cimon's family

During the period of the Persian wars and the rebuilding of Athens, a young man named Cimon was growing up in Athens. He was born in about 512 B.C.

Cimon's father was Miltiades. Miltiades had been a successful general, and had commanded the victorious Athenian forces at the battle of Marathon against the Persians in 490 B.C. The following year he fell out of favour with the Athenians. On his recommendation the Athenians sent a naval expedition to capture the island of Paros; but under his command, the expedition was a failure. When he returned, he was charged with defrauding Athens, and would have been put to death, had it not been for his earlier achievements. As it was, he was fined heavily. He could not pay the fine immediately and so was kept in prison where he died from an injury he had received on the campaign. Cimon, still a young man with an unmarried sister Elpinice, was left fatherless, and poor as well, as a result of paying his father's fine.

Helmet dedicated by Miltiades, discovered at Olympia.

Plutarch
Cimon 4

For a while Cimon did nothing worth mentioning in public life; he just got a bad reputation for being drunk and disorderly. It is said that he did not receive any education in literature and music or anything else that freeborn Greeks are usually taught. Unlike most Athenians, he was neither a clever man nor a fluent public speaker. However, his good birth and his honesty apparently showed in his face, and there was something about the simplicity of his character that was Spartan rather than Athenian.

While he was still a young man, he was accused of having had an incestuous relationship with his sister. Elpinice is said to have had affairs

13

with other men, too, including Polygnotus the painter. (This is what lies behind the story that he included the face of Elpinice when he was painting the Trojan women in the building called the Painted Stoa.) Other people have said that there was nothing secret about Elpinice's relationship with Cimon; they said that she lived with him quite openly as his wife, because she was too poor to find a husband to match her high birth. They add that Callias, one of the wealthiest men in Athens, fell in love with her. He offered to marry her and pay Cimon the money for her father's fine. Elpinice accepted, and Cimon gave her away in marriage to Callias.

However that may be, it is clear that Cimon fell in love with women very easily. He was, if anything, too devoted to Isodice, his lawful wife. When she died, he was distraught, judging by an elegy written to console him in his grief.

III.2   Cimon's character and appearance

Plutarch
Cimon 5 We can admire all the other aspects of Cimon's character. He was as courageous as Miltiades, he had as much understanding as Themistocles, and it is agreed that he had a greater sense of justice than either of them. He was just as much of an expert in war as they were, but incalculably better as a statesman, even when he was still a young man without any experience in war.

When the Persians invaded Greece, Themistocles tried to persuade the people to give up their city and leave their land. Instead, Themistocles argued, they should join their fleet off the island of Salamis and fight it out at sea. Most people were frightened out of their minds at the boldness of the plan, but Cimon was the first to be seen going up to the Acropolis, in a cheerful frame of mind and with a group of friends. He was carrying his horse's bridle to dedicate to the goddess, since he wanted to show that at that time the city needed not the strength of cavalry but men to fight a sea-battle. When he had dedicated the bridle, he took one of the shields that had been hung up around the temple, and offered up a prayer to the goddess. He then want down to the sea. As a result of this gesture, there was a great improvement in morale.

There was nothing to find fault with in his appearance either. He was tall, with thick curly hair. And when he actually fought at Salamis, he was spectacularly heroic, so that he soon won both glory and affection among the Athenians. He came under considerable pressure from throngs of admirers to mastermind and put in motion immediately some scheme equal to Marathon. So on his entry to public life, the people gave him a warm welcome. They had had more than enough of Themistocles, and promoted Cimon to the position of highest honour and responsibility in the state. What appealed to them most was his mild manner and openness. 480 B.C.

Plutarch says that the man who advanced Cimon's career most at this stage was Aristeides. Aristeides had taken a prominent part in the Persian Wars, being a leader at Marathon, Salamis and Plataea. He had the reputation of being an honest, old-fashioned aristocrat, and may have felt that Cimon's style of leadership would be similar.

III.3   A new leader for the Greeks

Cimon was given the chance to further his military career when he and Aristeides led the Athenian section of the Greek allied troops. Although the Persians had been driven from the Greek mainland in 479 B.C., the Greeks still needed to send out expeditions to free the Greeks in Ionia on the edge of the Persian empire. The Spartan Pausanias was in overall command of the Greek allies at this time.

Plutarch Cimon 6; Aristeides 23

The soldiers whom Cimon provided for these campaigns were not only outstanding for their discipline but were also much keener than the others. The Athenians were popular with the Greek allies because Aristeides was so fair and Cimon was so reasonable. The allies began to favour the Athenians as their leaders, and were influenced further in this by Pausanias' greed and severity.

At that time Pausanias was turning traitor. He was scheming with the enemy and sending letters to the king of Persia, while his own allies were putting up with his cruel and overbearing behaviour. The commanders met with bad temper and cruelty, while he punished ordinary soldiers by flogging them and making them hold up an iron anchor all day. None of them were allowed to provide their horses with bedding or hay, or fetch water from the spring before the Spartans had done so. If they tried to do so, the Spartans' slaves would drive them away with whips.

Cimon, on the other hand, welcomed the people who had been unjustly treated and handled them so sympathetically that he became the leader of the Greeks almost without their realising it. This was achieved not by force of arms, but by the way he spoke and behaved. This led most of the allies to follow Aristeides and Cimon, since they could not put up with being badly treated and despised by Pausanias. As soon as Aristeides and Cimon had won over the allies, they sent a message to the Spartans telling them to recall Pausanias. They said that he had disgraced Sparta and disrupted the Greek action.

The Spartans duly recalled Pausanias. They sent out no more generals, and so gave up their leadership of the allies. Nor did they take any further part in the alliance of the Greeks against the Persians.

III.4   New terms for the alliance

Thucydides I.96; Plutarch Aristeides 2–5

Even when the Spartans were leading them, the Greeks had paid something towards the cost of the war against Persia, but now they wanted each city to be assessed fairly. To this end they asked the Athenians for

478–476 B.C.

15

Aristeides, and instructed him to make a survey of each city's land and its wealth, and then to fix a rate of payment according to each city's assets and ability to pay. So the Athenians laid down which cities should provide money and which should provide ships. The idea was to carry out raids into the king of Persia's territory, and in this way make good any losses they had suffered through the war. The money that was contributed by the states was called tribute, and at first the total was fixed at 460 talents. The alliance that was formed in this way had its treasury on the island of Delos, and meetings of representatives of the member states were held in the temple there.

Aristeides was poor when he started this task of organising the alliance's finances, and although he was given such absolute power, and although in a way Greece entrusted all her property to him alone, he was even poorer when he had finished. He avoided bribery and his assessment of the tribute to be paid by each city was fair. In fact, all the states felt that he was their friend and that his scheme suited them perfectly.

Aristeides bound the Greeks with an oath. He swore the oath for the Athenians himself and to seal it he threw red-hot wedges of iron into the sea.

Because its treasury was at Delos, historians call this alliance the Delian League. Over the next ten years (477 to 467 B.C.), the League sent out campaigns to remove the threat of further Persian invasions and make the Aegean safe for shipping.

In 476 B.C. Cimon led the allies against Eion in Thrace, which was under Persian occupation. They captured the city but there was nothing left worth taking, since the Persians had set fire to it at the last minute. However, since the land was very fertile, Cimon handed it over to the Athenians.

Cimon then captured the island of Scyros. The people who lived on the island had made their living out of piracy, so by enslaving them Cimon cleared the Aegean sea of pirates. He does not seem to have been general for a number of years after this. There was also a war in Euboea. One of the cities there, Carystus, was still loyal to Persia, but now it was brought into the League with the rest of Euboea.

III.5   Changes in the Delian League

Plutarch
Cimon 11

Athens' allies were still paying the agreed sums of money into the fund for the war against Persia, but they did not supply the proper number of men or ships. They had now had enough of military service: they could see no need for fighting, and were anxious instead to farm their land and lead a quiet life, now that the barbarians had left them alone. The Athenian generals tried to force them to keep to the terms of the alliance by fining them and punishing them. The result was that the allies detested the burden of Athenian rule.

When Cimon was general, he treated the allies very differently from the way other generals had done. If any allies did not want to do military service, he did not force them; instead he just accepted money and ships with crews from them. So these allies were ensnared by their taste for leisure: Cimon let them spend their time on their own affairs so that they became peaceful farmers and merchants instead of soldiers. On the other hand, he made large numbers of the Athenians take turns at serving as ships' crews and toughened them up on expeditions. In a short time they were superior to the allies, even though it was the allies who had supplied the money for their wages. The allies who did no military service began to fear the Athenians and wanted to keep on the right side of them, because they were always at sea, fighting or training. They did not notice that instead of allies they had now become slaves paying tribute.

III.6   Naxos rebels

Thucydides
I.98–9
Some time later the island of Naxos left the alliance and Athens went to war against it. Naxos was besieged and forced back into the alliance, and so became the first allied state to lose her freedom. This was against the constitution of the alliance, but the same thing happened to other states for various reasons. The Athenians were no longer such popular rulers as they had been. They did more than their share of fighting, and that made it easier for them to force any rebellious states back into the alliance.

467
B.C.

III.7   Action against the Persians

Meanwhile the allies were making further expeditions against the Persians, under the leadership of the Athenians.

Plutarch
Cimon 12
It was Cimon who did more than anyone else to cut the Persian king down to size and quell his pride. He did not let the Persians just withdraw from Greece, but followed hard on their heels. Before they could stop to draw breath, he was destroying and overthrowing some cities, and making others rebel and come over to the Greeks' side so that the whole of Ionia was completely free of Persian soldiers.

Cimon wanted to make the Persians too afraid even to enter Greek seas; so when he heard that the king's generals were lying in wait for him on the coast of Pamphylia with a large army and many ships, he set sail with 200 triremes. He put in at the city of Phaselis, but although the people there were Greeks they refused to let in his troops or to desert the Persian king. Cimon plundered their land and attacked their walls. However, Cimon's fleet included troops from Chios, who were old friends of the people of Phaselis. They tried to calm Cimon down, and at the same time they attached little messages to arrows which they shot over the wall to tell the people of Phaselis what was going on. In the end Cimon made peace on condition that the people of Phaselis should pay ten talents and follow him in his campaign against the Persians.

The battle at the river Eurymedon

c.467 B.C.

The Persians were waiting for 80 more ships to arrive and were not at all keen to face the Greeks, so they retreated up the river Eurymedon. However, when the Greeks pursued them, they sailed out and fought against them with a large fleet.

Plutarch Cimon 12

In the sea battle the Persians' large force did not live up to expectations: they turned back immediately and made for the shore. The first to reach the land took refuge among the foot soldiers, who were drawn up nearby. The Greeks overtook others and destroyed both them and their ships. There must have been a very great number of barbarians' ships which took part in the action: although many seem to have escaped and many were destroyed, the Athenians still captured 200.

Plutarch Cimon 13

The Persian foot soldiers marched down to the sea, but Cimon thought it would be too much to make a forced landing, and then lead his exhausted men against troops who had not yet fought and who far outnumbered them. But he saw that his men were in high spirits because of the strength and courage they had gained from the victory. They were keen to fight hand-to-hand with the barbarians, so he put his hoplites* ashore. Still hot from their fighting in the sea-battle, they ran at the enemy with a shout. The Persians stood firm and faced the attackers heroically and a fierce battle followed. Some of the bravest and highest-ranking Athenians fell in the battle, but after a massive struggle they turned the Persians back, killing as they went. They took captives and seized the camp which was full of all kinds of treasures.

Cimon won two victories in a single day, but this did not stop him concluding the expedition with yet another. Before returning home, he sailed against the 80 ships that the Persians had been waiting for at the Eurymedon. According to Plutarch, all the ships were destroyed along with their crews.

III.8 Money in hand

Plutarch Cimon 10

Cimon was now very well off. He had money in hand from fighting the enemy and people thought that this was greatly to his credit. He was now in a position to spend the proceeds on his fellow citizens, and that was even more to his credit. He removed the fences from his fields so that outsiders as well as poor Athenians would feel free to help themselves to his produce. He also laid on a meal at his home every day. It was not extravagant but there was enough for a lot of people. Any poor citizen who wanted to could

*hoplites. Regular Greek heavy-armed foot-soldiers.

take advantage of this offer of a free meal, so that he could concentrate on taking his share in the running of the state without having to worry about keeping himself. However, Aristotle says that Cimon provided this meal only for the people of his own district, not for all Athenians.

Cimon always went around with a group of young men wearing good clothes. If he met an elderly citizen in need of better clothes, one of the young men would swap cloaks with him. This custom was seen as a great act of charity. The same young men also carried with them a good supply of cash. They would go up to the poor but respectable people in the Agora* and discreetly put some small change into their hands.

And so in a way Cimon made it possible for people to experience the sort of life described in the stories about the Golden Age, when men owned everything in common. There were slanderers who made out that Cimon was only doing all this to please the common people and win them over; however, they were proved wrong by Cimon's political views which were in sympathy with the aristocracy and Sparta. In fact, together with Aristeides, he opposed Themistocles who was trying to give the people excessive power. Also, although he saw that everyone was making a profit out of public office, except for a few like Aristeides, he neither received nor offered bribes in the course of his duty; he was upright to the end in all he did and said, without looking for any reward.

Plutarch
Cimon 13

The goods captured from the Persians were sold. As a result, the Athenians had money for various things, and in particular, they built the southern wall of the Acropolis. It is said, too, that although the Long Walls

*Agora. The market-place and civic centre of a Greek city.

The South Wall of the Acropolis. On the top of the Acropolis can be seen Athene's temple, the Parthenon. It was not there in Cimon's day, and the walls of the Acropolis have been substantially altered through the ages.

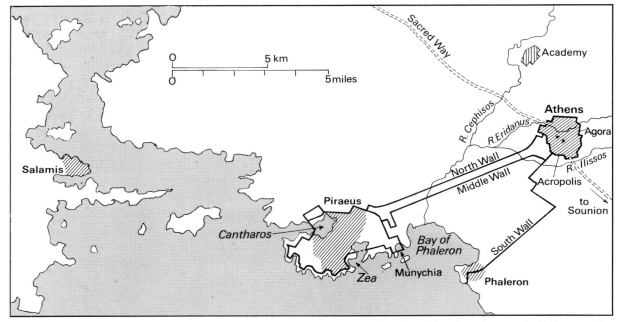

Athens and its harbours, showing the 'Long Walls' as completed. The North and South walls were built first and the middle later. Phaleron, a wide sweeping bay, was the port of Athens before Peiraeus was developed.

were actually finished later, Cimon laid the first secure foundations. The work was held up by swamps and marshes, and Cimon himself paid for large quantities of rubble and heavy stone to be tipped into the swamps. He was also the first to beautify the city, by planting plane trees in the Agora, and by changing the Academy★ from a dry, burnt-up place into an elegant wooded area with springs where he provided open running-tracks and shady places to walk. These amenities soon became extremely popular.

★*Academy*. A park on the outskirts of Athens named after the hero Academus. It gave its name to a college founded there by the philosopher Plato, about 385 B.C. From this comes the modern word *academy*.

Water pipe discovered in the Agora, near to the Painted Stoa. Other sections have been found, all leading in the direction of the Academy.

IV Early life of Pericles and the later career of Cimon

This chapter starts in about 495 B.C., when Pericles was born in Athens some years after Cimon.

IV.1 Pericles' family and education

Both sides of Pericles' family were well-known and respected: his father Xanthippus had defeated the Persian generals at Mycale in 479 B.C.; his mother Agariste was the niece of Cleisthenes (see Introduction p.9)

Head inscribed with Pericles' name. (Roman copy of Greek original.)

Plutarch
Pericles 3

Agariste dreamt that she had given birth to a lion and a few days later she had Pericles. Pericles' appearance was almost perfect, except for his head, which was too long. Because of this, artists almost always portrayed him wearing a helmet, as if they did not want to make fun of this defect.

507 B.C.

Pericles would have received the usual basic education in athletics, music and the works of the ancient poets (especially Homer). He also received advanced education in philosophy and the art of debate from well-known teachers or 'sophists'. One of these was Zeno, who taught Pericles to defeat his opponents by clever cross-questioning. Plutarch recalls the following story about Pericles' skill in this.

Plutarch
Pericles 8

A story told by Thucydides the son of Melesias has come down to us. It was meant as a joke, but it proves how persuasive Pericles could be. Thucydides was on the side of the aristocrats and was Pericles' opponent in politics for a very long time. Archidamus, the king of Sparta, once asked him whether he or Pericles was better at wrestling. Thucydides replied: 'Whenever I throw him in wrestling, he wins all the same – by arguing that he was never thrown! He even makes the people watching him believe him.'

The teacher whom Pericles admired most was Anaxagoras. As well as affecting the way he thought, Anaxagoras influenced his manner and his style of public speaking.

Plutarch
Pericles 5

As a result, Pericles became serious-minded and his style of speech was dignified, with none of the vulgar language and unfair tactics of orators who tried to win over the mob. His face never creased with laughter, he moved quietly, his cloak was carefully arranged so that it never slipped out of position while he was speaking and the tone of his voice was controlled. These and other signs of his self-restraint astounded everyone. There is a true story about this. On one occasion, some vulgar layabout called him names and insulted him for the whole day. Pericles just put up with it without saying a word, even though he was in the Agora at the time with pressing business to deal with. Towards evening he returned home, dignified as ever, while the man stuck to him, still piling on every kind of offensive remark. Pericles was about to go into his house when he ordered one of his slaves to take a light, as it was now dark, and to accompany the man back to his own house.

In contrast to this view of Pericles, the poet Ion says that he was rather high-handed and stuck-up in his dealings with people, and while taking pride in himself he looked down on others. On the other hand, Ion praises Cimon for being pleasant, easy-going and cultivated as he went about his business. However, we can forget about Ion: he thinks that a good man must have a bit of the clown in him, just as a set of tragic plays is not complete without a comedy at the end.

IV.2   Pericles and the people

Plutarch
Pericles 7–8
When Pericles was a young man, he took care to avoid the Assembly. One reason for this was that people thought he looked very like the tyrant Peisistratus; men who were old enough to remember Peisistratus were much stuck by the likeness: 'What a nice voice he has!' they said, 'and how well he talks!' Another reason was that he was afraid of being ostracised.*
This was because he was rich and came from a famous family and had friends in high places. He therefore took no part in politics, but became a soldier instead and showed tremendous courage and daring.

But there came a time when Aristeides was dead, Themistocles had been banished, and Cimon's campaigns kept him outside Greece most of the time. It was then that Pericles went over to the people's side, choosing the poor and the masses instead of the rich minority. This was against his nature which was not in the least in sympathy with the people. It looks as though he was afraid that people would think he was aiming to become sole ruler; and when he saw that Cimon was on the side of the upper classes and was exceedingly popular with the traditional ruling families, he began trying to win the favour of the masses. He did this both to protect himself and to gain power to use against Cimon.

Pericles now adopted a different life-style. There was only one street in the city where he was to be seen walking – the street that led to the Agora and the council-chamber. He would have nothing to do with invitations to dinner or similar opportunities for being friendly and sociable. He also made sure that he was not seen so often, even by the people, that they became bored with him: instead of speaking to them on every matter, he addressed them only occasionally, keeping himself in reserve for real crises.

*ostracised. Ostracism was a form of banishment.

An Athenian cup showing a dinner party. (490—480 B.C.)

He carried out the rest of his policy by putting it into the hands of his friends and other public speakers.

It is certainly true that Pericles chose his words carefully, and whenever he stepped onto the platform to speak, he prayed to the gods that he might not let slip any word out of tune with the matter in hand.

IV.3 Cimon on trial

One of the first things we know about Pericles is the part he played when Cimon was put on trial by the Athenian people. This came about in the following way.

Thucydides 1.100

Some time after Cimon had defeated the Persians at the Eurymedon, the island of Thasos revolted from the Delian League. The reason was an argument over trade in mainland Thrace and over a mine controlled by Thasos.

465 B.C.

Plutarch *Cimon* 14

Cimon defeated the Thasians at sea and captured thirty-three ships. He then besieged their city until it surrendered and seized for Athens the gold mines on the mainland opposite and the land there which had been ruled by the Thasians.

The Athenians thought that this foothold in Thrace would have given Cimon the chance to march on into Macedonia and seize a large slice of land. But he did not want to do this, and so the Athenians said he must have been bribed by the king of Macedonia, and his enemies in Athens joined forces to bring a case against him. When he was defending himself at the trial he said to the jury, 'There are other Athenians who are paid by rich Ionians or Thessalians to act in their interests, Athenians who look for flattery and rewards from such people. Am I that sort of Athenian? No! It

23

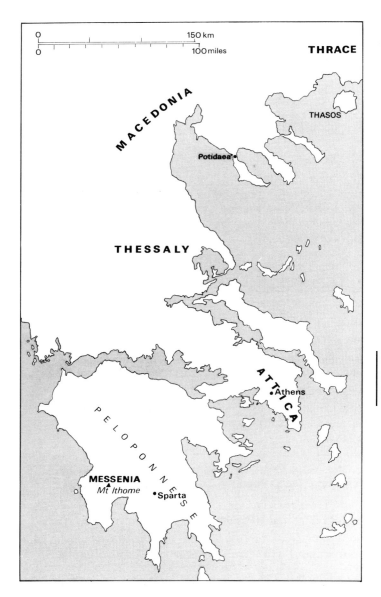

is the Spartans that I would act for. My model is their simple and restrained way of life and I'm glad of it! Give me these qualities any day rather than wealth. Yes, I do have wealth, but I spend it on our city – and I won it from our enemies.'

There is a story that when Pericles had been chosen as one of Cimon's ten prosecutors, Cimon's sister Elpinice helped to tone down Pericles' attack on him. She came to plead with him, but Pericles smiled and said, 'Elpinice, you are an old lady, too old for this sort of thing.' However, he only made one speech, which was all he was obliged to do, and finished up by doing less harm to Cimon than the rest of the prosecutors.

Cimon was heavily fined but was acquitted of the charge of treason. The admiration he had expressed for the Spartans was nothing new.

IV.4 Cimon and the Spartans

Plutarch
Cimon 16

It is true that right from the start of his career Cimon was very pro-Spartan. He actually gave two of his sons Spartan names. At first, the Athenians were pleased to see this, because the friendliness of the Spartans was very useful to them. This was in the early days of their empire when they were still busy making alliances, and they were happy to see Cimon in an honoured and favoured position. He was their leading statesman, since he treated their allies sympathetically and was well-liked by the Spartans.

Later, however, when the Athenians had become powerful, they were annoyed to see how deeply involved with the Spartans Cimon was. At every opportunity he tended to tell the Athenians how wonderful the Spartans were, especially when he was criticising the Athenians or urging them on. We are told that he would say, 'But the Spartans aren't like that.' This led to his being resented and disliked by the Athenians.

IV.5 Crisis at Sparta, changes at Athens

It was Cimon's support for Sparta that helped to bring about his downfall. The events leading up to this were as follows.

An earthquake and a rebellion

When the people of Thasos were under siege from the Athenians, the Spartans had promised to help them by invading Attica. However, they were prevented from doing so by troubles at home: there was a severe earthquake, and at the same time (464 B.C.) the helots* rebelled, making a base for themselves at Mount Ithome. As a result, Sparta now badly needed help herself.

Thucydides
I.102

The war at Ithome was dragging on, so the Spartans asked their allies, including Athens, to send help. They were particularly keen to have help from the Athenians because the Athenians were said to be skilled at siegecraft. This siege had been going on for a long time, so it was obvious to the Spartans that they themselves were not as competent in this type of warfare or they would have stormed the place by now.

The Athenians discussed the Spartans' request for help in the Assembly. One of the speakers was Ephialtes. He had fought under Cimon at the battle of the Eurymedon, but was opposed to the power of aristocrats, such as Cimon, in the government.

Plutarch
Cimon 16

Ephialtes wanted to refuse the request. 'Men of Athens,' he said, 'Sparta is your rival. Don't come to her rescue, and don't put her back on her feet. Leave her lying where she is, and while she's lying there stamp on her as well!'

But Cimon considered what was best for Sparta instead of what would make his own city more powerful, and he persuaded the Athenians to send a large force of hoplites to help the Spartans. The very words by which Cimon influenced them most have come down to us: 'Do not let Greece go lame, do not let this city of ours become a one-horse chariot.'

'Undiluted democracy'

Cimon set off for Ithome with 400 hoplites. Meanwhile Ephialtes took advantage of their absence and brought about changes in the way Athens was governed.

helots. The Spartans' slaves.

25

Plutarch *Cimon* 15

The people were making inroads into the rights of the nobles and trying to get positions in the government and gain power for themselves. While he was in Athens, Cimon managed to get the better of them and put them back in their place. But when he sailed away on a military expedition, the people broke out completely. Up to that time they had always followed the accepted way of running the state and the traditions of their ancestors. But now they threw all this into confusion, and following Ephialtes' lead they took away from the Council of the Areopagus all but a few of the types of case it had handled. They put themselves in charge of the law-courts and sent the city headlong into undiluted democracy.

462 B.C.

Plutarch *Cimon* 15; *Pericles* 9

Pericles, too, was involved, since he was now a powerful man and the ally of the people. He did not have the wealth and resources to win over the poor as Cimon had done, so instead he decided to make public money available to the people. He gave grants for festivals, wages for jurors and other payments and hand-outs, and soon he had bought for himself the total support of the people and used it to undermine the Council of the Areopagus, of which he was not a member.

IV.6 Cimon's downfall

While these changes in the form of government were taking place in Athens, Cimon's expedition to help the Spartans at Ithome was not going smoothly.

Thucydides I.102

This expedition to Ithome was the first occasion that Athens and Sparta quarrelled openly. Ithome had not yet fallen and the Spartans became afraid of the Athenians because of their initiative and their strange new ways of doing things. 'The Athenians are foreigners after all', they said to themselves. 'If they stay in the Peloponnese, they might be persuaded by our enemies at Ithome to join in an uprising against us.' So, while accepting the help of their other allies, they sent the Athenians away. They did not say outright that they were suspicious; they just said that they did not need the Athenians any more. The Athenians, however, realised that they were not being dismissed for this reason, but that they were under suspicion.

Plutarch *Cimon* 15

Cimon came home to find that the people had made a mockery of the Areopagus, as a respected council. He was furious. He tried to restore its importance as a law-court and to bring back the old aristocratic form of government, but the leaders of the people united to denounce him. They also tried to make the people angry with him; so they brought up the old scandals about his relations with his sister and accused him of being too fond of Sparta.

Plutarch *Cimon* 17

The Athenians came back from Ithome feeling very angry. They were now openly hostile to all supporters of Sparta and especially to Cimon. They ostracised him for ten years, finding some feeble excuse for their action.

461 B.C.

V The First Peloponnesian War and the growth of Athenian power

V.1 New alliances

After Cimon was ostracised the Athenians completely gave up cooperating with Sparta and her allies. During this period, known as the First Peloponnesian War, they made sure of their fortifications by completing the Long Walls between Athens and Piraeus, protecting the port and keeping open access to the sea. They also came into conflict with Corinth. Corinth was an ally of Sparta and was in an important position, controlling the passage between Attica and the Peloponnese.

Thucydides I.102

The Athenians broke off the alliance with Sparta which had been made against Persia, and became the allies of Sparta's enemy Argos.

461 B.C.

Thucydides I.103

It was at this time, too, that Megara joined the Athenian alliance. The Megarians broke off their alliance with Sparta because the Corinthians were attacking them in a war over the boundaries between them. In this

Central Greece

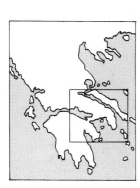

way the Athenians held Megara and Pagae, and they built long walls for the Megarians from their city to the port of Nisaea. These were guarded by Athenian troops. This was the main reason why the Corinthians began to hate the Athenians so much.

Various disputes followed. Maritime centres such as Corinth and the island of Aegina were becoming more and more concerned about Athens' naval power. Eventually (about 459 B.C.), the Athenians found themselves involved in three different wars:
1 Aegina revolted from the alliance. The Athenians besieged it.
2 The Corinthians marched on Megara, hoping to draw the Athenians away from Aegina. The Athenians sent an army against them. The Corinthians were defeated and the siege of Aegina continued.
3 Athenian troops were also sent to Egypt in an attempt to liberate it from Persian rule.

V.2   The battle of Tanagra

Meanwhile the Spartans were fighting in Doris, as they were involved in a dispute between two cities there. The fighting stopped when Sparta forced the two cities to make peace.

Thucydides I.107–8

The Spartans then began to think how to return home. If they went by sea, the Athenians would sail round with their fleet and stop them. The route overland did not seem to them to be safe either, because Athens held Megara and Pagae. In any case, the passes were difficult and were constantly guarded by the Athenians.

The Spartans therefore decided to stay in Boeotia. They could wait there and see what would be the safest route by which to march home. Another reason for acting cautiously was that a group of people in Athens was hoping to put a stop both to the democracy in Athens and to the building of the Long Walls, and were secretly negotiating with the Spartans for their help.

The Athenians had the idea that the Spartans were in difficulties over their passage home. They also suspected that there was a plot against the democracy. So, with the help of their allies, including 1,000 troops from Argos, they marched against the Spartans with their whole force – 14,000 men altogether.

457 B.C.

Plutarch Pericles 10

Cimon, too, came back from exile, and took his place in the fighting force with the men of his tribe. By fighting in the battle and taking his share of the danger facing his fellow citizens, he wanted to remove all suspicion that he was on Sparta's side.

Plutarch Cimon 17

But the Council of Five Hundred found out about this and were very alarmed. What Cimon really wanted to do, his enemies said, was to unsettle the army and then lead the Spartans against Athens. The Council therefore told the generals not to accept him. Cimon went away, but he urged those of his friends whom people most suspected of being pro-Spartan to put up a good fight against the enemy and by their deeds prove wrong those citizens who had suspected them.

Thucydides
I.108

The battle was fought at Tanagra in Boeotia. Many men fell on both sides, and the Spartans and their allies were the victors.

V.3   Cimon recalled

Plutarch
Cimon 17

Cimon's friends had taken his armour to the battle at Tanagra and set it up in their ranks. Shoulder to shoulder, they threw themselves into the fighting. All one hundred of them were killed. The Athenians were left with an overwhelming sense of loss and remorse at having accused the men unjustly. As a result, anger against Cimon was soon forgotten, partly because they remembered the good things he had done. This was only natural, but in addition the course of events helped him back into favour. After all, the Athenians had suffered a defeat in the important battle at Tanagra and expected that a Spartan army would attack them in the spring. So they recalled Cimon from exile. In fact, the decree which brought about his recall was proposed by Pericles. This shows the extent to which arguments in those days were on a political level; personal feelings were suppressed to fit in with the public interest.

There is little evidence for Cimon's career between 461 B.C. and 451 B.C. Plutarch mentions his ostracism and early recall in both the *Life of Cimon* and the *Life of Pericles*. However, there is no other evidence that he was active in Athenian affairs before 451.

Hoplite armour on a vase made early in the fifth century B.C. Not shown are the bronze greaves and spear, which was about 2.75m (9') long.

V.4 Gains and losses

Thucydides
I.108

Sixty-two days after the battle of Tanagra, the Athenians marched into Boeotia. They defeated the Boeotians and took control of the whole of Boeotia. They removed Tanagra's city walls, and took as hostages a hundred of the wealthiest people from among those they had conquered. Meanwhile they finished building their own Long Walls.

A little while later, Aegina surrendered. The Athenians made her destroy her city walls, hand over her fleet and ordered her to pay tribute in future.

457 B.C.

The Athenians also sailed round the Peloponnese, burning the Spartan shipyards and capturing one of Corinth's subject cities. They then landed at Sicyon and defeated the people of Sicyon in battle.

455 B.C.

These actions strengthened Athens' position, especially in the Gulf of Corinth. However, the expedition to free Egypt from Persian rule ended in disaster, with heavy losses of men and ships.

Pericles led another expedition along the Peloponnesian coast, using Pagae as a base. He won another battle at Sicyon, but did not capture any other towns.

The failure of the Egyptian expedition made the Persian threat seem greater. On these grounds, Athens declared that the League treasury on Delos was not secure enough.

Tribute list for the year 440/439.

The Athenians, who were still in command of the sea, removed to Athens the money which had been collected in Delos for the benefit of all the allies. This amounted to about 8,000 talents and it was handed over to Pericles to look after.

454 B.C.

One-sixtieth of the money collected from the allies each year was dedicated to the goddess Athene and this was recorded on stone tablets. These survive in part and provide the evidence for the amount of tribute collected at different times and the names of the communities who had to pay it.

V.5   Peace with Sparta and the death of Cimon

Three years later in 451 B.C., a five-year truce between the Spartans and the Athenians brought the First Peloponnesian War to a close. Once more under the command of Cimon, the Athenians revived their action against Persia and her allies.

Thucydides I.112

Because they did not have to fight a war in Greece, the Athenians, under the command of Cimon, sailed against Cyprus with 200 ships, some of them their own and some provided by their allies. Sixty of these were sent off to Egypt. With the rest of the ships, the Athenians besieged Cition. However, they were forced to abandon the siege because of Cimon's death and because their supplies were running out.

Plutarch gives a more detailed account of this campaign and Cimon's death.

Plutarch *Cimon* 18–19

While Cimon was holding his fleet near to Cyprus and thinking about these ambitious plans for conquest, he sent messengers to the shrine of Ammon to ask the oracle there a secret question. Nobody knows what this question was. The god made no reply, but as the messengers approached, the oracle told them to depart again, saying, 'Cimon himself is already with me.'

When they heard these words, the messengers went back to the sea. They reached the Greek camp, which was on the coast of Egypt at that time, and were told that Cimon was dead. They counted the days back to the time when the oracle had spoken to them and then they understood the riddle: the oracle had said that Cimon was with the gods because he was dead.

449 B.C.

Most people say that Cimon died of some disease while he was besieging Cition, but others say that he died from a wound that he suffered in a battle with the Persians. As he was dying, he instructed his men to sail away immediately and pretend that he was still alive. And so it happened that neither the Greek allies nor the enemy were aware of what had happened. It was reported that the expedition was brought back safely 'with Cimon as general', although he had been dead for thirty days.

Cimon's remains were brought back to Athens. This is proved by the monuments commemorating him which to this day are named after him.

449 B.C.

Relations with Persia were not a major problem after this time. Fifth-century writers do not mention a formal peace treaty, but later writers say that one was arranged by Callias, Cimon's brother-in-law. At any rate, there were no more expeditions against Persia, but even so the Delian League still existed, with Athens at its head. Gaps in the Tribute Lists suggest that there was a brief interval when tribute was not collected but then the allies found themselves paying money to Athens just as before.

V.6   Pericles opposed

Plutarch
Pericles 11

The aristocrats had known for some time that the foremost citizen was now Pericles. They were keen to have someone who would be his opponent in the city – someone who would blunt the sharp edge of his power so that they would not be ruled by one man. So they set up against him a man called Thucydides,* who had a lot of sense and was a relative of Cimon. He was not a soldier like Cimon, but was more of a public figure and a politician. He kept an eye on what was happening in the city and entered into debate with Pericles, and so he soon brought about a proper balance in the way the city was run.

Up to now the aristocrats had been scattered in the Assembly, merging with the masses so that their impact was weakened. Thucydides would not allow this. Instead he separated out the aristocrats and brought them together in one group so that they carried more weight. It was like making scales balance.

In the life of Athens, there had always been a sort of seam or rift below the surface, like a fault in a piece of iron. This was a sign of the difference between the people and the aristocrats. But now the ambition and rivalry of Pericles and Thucydides opened up this fault into a deep cut in the state, so that one side was called 'the people' and the other side 'the few'.

Because of this, Pericles made a point at this time of handing over the reins of government to the people and putting forward policies which would appeal to them. He was forever laying on some kind of spectacular festival in the city or a feast or a procession, amusing the people like children with sophisticated entertainments. He also sent out 1,750 Athenians to settle in various parts of Greece, and others to found a new colony in South Italy called Thurii. In this way he stopped the city being weighed down with all those who were lazy and had time on their hands to cause trouble; he eased the people's poverty; and the garrisons that he established among the neighbours brought with them fear of what would happen if they were to rebel.

*The politician mentioned earlier (IV.1).

V.7 Temples for all time

Plutarch
Pericles 12–13

But there was one thing above all which brought delight and beauty to the city of Athens and amazement to the rest of mankind; something which is our only evidence that the ancient power and glory of Greece are not just fiction. By this I mean the construction of the temples to the gods.

It was this measure of Pericles which his enemies slandered most of all. They attacked him in the Assembly and shouted out that the people of Athens had lost their good name and disgraced themselves by transferring the common funds of the Greeks from Delos and using them as their own. The Athenian people used to have a good excuse: they used to say that they were afraid that the Persians would steal the funds, and so they were keeping them in a safe place. But now Pericles had destroyed that excuse. His actions were a dreadful insult to the rest of Greece and an act of bare-faced tyranny. People who had been forced to make contributions to the war now had to see the Athenians using the money to decorate and beautify the city, like a woman tarting herself up with precious stones, statues, and temples costing millions.

Pericles informed the people that they did not need to give any account of the money to their allies, provided that they carried on the war for them and kept the barbarians away.

'They don't provide a single horse, ship or hoplite. All they give is money, and this doesn't belong to the people who give it. It belongs to those who receive it – provided they supply the things they've been paid for. If the city has been fully equipped with everything she needs for the war, then it's only right that any extra funds should be used for projects which will bring her eternal glory when they are completed. There will be all sorts of enterprises, with many different requirements. People will be inspired to use their skills, and employment will be found for all. The city will provide the wages. She can decorate and support herself out of her own resources.'

Certainly, those who were young and fit could always earn a good living from public funds by going on military expeditions. But Pericles also wanted to give a share of the revenue to the common labourers who did not serve in the army. Since he did not want them to be paid for sitting about doing nothing, he put before the people some bold proposals for building projects which would require many skills and take some time to complete. His idea was that those who stayed at home should have as much of a claim to the benefits of public wealth as those who served as sailors, guards or soldiers.

The materials to be used were stone, bronze, ivory, gold, ebony and cypress-wood, and the skills needed to work them were those of the carpenter, painter, embroiderer and engraver. Then there were people who transported and supplied these materials. At sea, there were merchants, sailors, and people to steer the boats; on land there were waggon-makers, people to train the animals and people to drive them. There were also ropemakers, weavers, leather workers, road builders and miners. And just as a general has his own army, each of these skills had its own gang of organised labourers. So it would be true to say that the Athenians divided up and spread their wealth amongst people of every age and of every type.

The main reason why Pericles' works are so much admired is this: they were built in a short time, but they were built for all time. Each one was so beautiful that as soon as it was made it was treasured like an antique, yet each possesses such a freshness that it seems as if it were made only yesterday. They bloom with an eternal newness, untouched by time, as if someone had breathed into them the spirit of everlasting youth.

Aerial view of the Acropolis. The Parthenon (in the centre) and the Propylaea or gateway (to the left) were initiated by Pericles.

VI Worsening relations

VI.1 Trouble with the allies

Despite Athens' efforts to keep the allies under control, trouble broke out. Some of Athens' political opponents led an uprising in Boeotia. The Athenian army was defeated and had to give up Boeotia. Meanwhile there was unrest in other places too.

447 B.C.

Thucydides I.114

Soon after this, Euboea revolted from Athens. Pericles had already made the crossing to Euboea with an Athenian army when he received a message: Megara had revolted and the Spartans were about to invade Attica. Megara was being helped in her rebellion by Corinth and other cities. Pericles quickly brought the army back from Euboea, but before long, the Spartans, commanded by their king, had marched into Attica and were plundering the land.

446 B.C.

Plutarch Pericles 22–23

Pericles did not dare to join battle against a large force of brave hoplites all anxious to fight. He noticed, however, that the king was a very young man; and because of this, the Spartans had sent with him a man called Cleandridas to keep an eye on him and to help him. Of all his advisers, it was Cleandridas on whom the king relied most. Pericles sounded out Cleandridas in secret; he soon bribed him and persuaded him to lead the Spartans out of Attica.

When Pericles presented his accounts for the campaign, he recorded that he had spent ten talents 'for necessary purposes'. The people accepted this without asking awkward questions or going into the matter further.

Thucydides I.114; Plutarch Pericles 23

Pericles then led the Athenians back over to Euboea and subdued the whole island. They laid down peace terms for the country except for the city of Histiaea. There they drove out the inhabitants and took possession of the land themselves. These were the only people to be treated so mercilessly, because they had captured an Athenian ship and killed its crew.

VI.2 Peace with Sparta

Thucydides I.115

Soon after the Athenians came back from Euboea, they made a peace treaty with Sparta and her allies, to last for thirty years. Athens gave back cities she had won from the Peloponnese, including Nisaea and Pagae.

445 B.C.

VI.3 Pericles is put to the test

In spite of the crisis over Euboea and the Spartans' invasion in 446 B.C., Athens continued the ambitious building programme she had begun in 448 B.C. Thucydides and his party were still opposed to it.

35

Plutarch
Pericles 14 Thucydides and those who shared his way of thinking kept on accusing Pericles. 'It's public money he's wasting,' they said, 'and money that comes into Athens' coffers goes out again in all this extravagance!'

Pericles therefore asked the people in the Assembly whether they thought he had spent too much. 'Much too much!' they replied. 'All right,' said Pericles, 'let's spend my own money, not yours. Of course, when the buildings are dedicated, the inscriptions will be in my own name, not yours.'

At this challenge from Pericles, the people shouted out that he was to take whatever he needed from the public funds and to spare no expense. This may have been because they admired his grand gesture, or it may have been that they did not want to be done out of the glory of the works. In the end, Pericles risked a test of ostracism with Thucydides. As a result, Thucydides was banished and the opposition to Pericles collapsed.

VI.4   The war with Samos

The island of Samos, though a subject ally of Athens, had managed to keep her own navy. In 440 B.C. Samos and Miletus were at war over a nearby city that they both claimed was theirs. Samos was winning the war when Athens ordered her to stop. She refused and revolted from the alliance. All ten generals of Athens including Pericles, were sent to deal with the crisis and they made the Samians set up a democratic form of government. A group in Samos then tried to overthrow the democracy with help from the Persians. The Athenians fought the Samians at sea and eventually besieged them.

Plutarch
Pericles 28 In the ninth month of the siege the Samians surrendered. Pericles destroyed their city walls, seized their warships and fined them heavily. They paid some of the money straightaway and they agreed to pay the rest at a fixed time, giving hostages as a guarantee.

Duris, the Samian writer, makes a tragedy of these events. He accuses the Athenians and Pericles of great brutality, which neither Thucydides nor other sources mention. But he does not seem to be telling the truth when he says: 'Pericles had the Samian captains and marines brought into the agora at Miletus and crucified there. After ten days of suffering, he ordered them to be removed, their heads to be beaten in with clubs and their bodies to be thrown out unburied.' But at the best of times Duris does not tend to be guided by strict truth in writing his accounts, even when he is not taking sides over a particular issue. It is therefore highly likely that in this case he has exaggerated the disasters that befell his country so that he can put the Athenians in a bad light.

When Pericles returned to Athens after he had defeated Samos, he had those who had been killed in the war buried with honour. He made the usual speech over the tombs, and this was greatly admired. As he came down from the platform women took his hand and crowned him with garlands and bands as though he were an athlete who had just won a victory. Elpinice, however, came up to him and said, 'This is splendid, Pericles, and you do so deserve these crowns. You have destroyed many brave citizens of ours – and you were not even fighting a war against the Persians, like my brother Cimon; you were putting down a Greek city, and an ally too.' It is said that Pericles ignored her remarks and made fun of her by quoting lines from a comic verse about mutton dressed as lamb, as if to say that she was too old to get round him.

VI.5   A love affair

Pericles had taken Miletus' side in the Samian War and this resulted in gossip about Pericles' relationship with Aspasia, a courtesan from Miletus who had the reputation of being very cultured and was widely respected for this by leading citizens and philosophers.

Plutarch
Pericles 24

According to some writers Pericles thought a great deal of Aspasia because of her excellent grasp of political matters. However, their relationship seems to have been more of a love affair. Pericles' wife was a close relation and had been married before. Her son from her previous marriage was Callias (known as Callias the Rich). By Pericles she had two sons. Later, when they found they did not get on well, Pericles gave her to another man, legally and with her consent, and he himself lived with Aspasia. He loved her very much and there is a story that on going out to the Agora and coming back again he would give her a kiss.

The only surviving statue of Aspasia which bears her name. (Roman copy of Greek original, found in 1777.)

VI.6   The approach of war

Relations between Athens, her allies and other Greek cities were becoming tense. Hostility between Athens and Sparta was increased and the peace treaty they had signed was put under strain as representatives of one city after another complained to Sparta that Athens was treating them badly. This was because Athens saw that war was coming and wanted to keep her existing allies under strict control and bring others over to her side.

The following accounts give some detail of the two most bitter disputes.

Corinth, Corcyra and Athens

Corcyra (modern Corfu) was a colony of Corinth, but relations between the two cities deteriorated as Corinth became jealous of Corcyra's growing naval power. They then fell out over how Corcyra's own colony should be governed, and this led to war between Corinth and Corcyra.

Both Corinth and Corcyra hoped that the Athenians would help them, so they sent representatives to Athens. This put Athens in a difficult position, as Corinth was an ally of Sparta with whom she had signed the treaty. Both sides put forward their argument to the Assembly.

Central and Northern Greece.

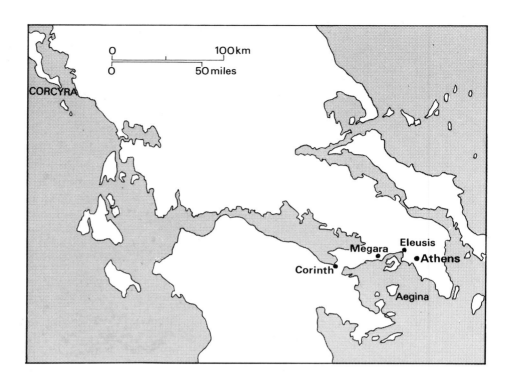

Thucydides
I.44

The Athenians listened to both sides and discussed the question at two meetings of the Assembly. At the first meeting, they seemed to favour the Corinthians' side, but at the seocnd they changed their minds and decided to make an alliance with Corcyra.

According to the terms of this alliance, Athens and Corcyra were not committed to supporting all of each other's friends and taking action against all of each other's enemies, for Athens would be breaking her treaty with Sparta if she had to join Corcyra in an attack on Corinth.

Most people felt that war with Sparta was bound to come, whatever they did. Athens did not want Corinth to get her hands on Corcyra's strong navy. Another point was Corcyra's position: it would be most useful to have an ally on the coastal route to Italy and Sicily.

Thucydides
I.45

The Athenians weighed up the situation and made an alliance with Corcyra. The Corinthian representatives went home. Soon afterwards, Athens sent ten ships to help Corcyra. Among their leaders was Lacedaemonius, Cimon's son. They had been told not to fight unless the Corinthians sailed against Corcyra with the idea of landing on the island itself or on any land belonging to Corcyra. If the Corinthians did sail against Corcyra, then they were to use force to stop them. They had been given these instructions to avoid breaking the treaty with Sparta.

Plutarch gives a different reason for the limited amount of help given to Corcyra. His version recalls the fact that Cimon gave his sons Spartan names. (Lacedaemonius means 'Spartan'.)

Plutarch *Pericles* 29

Pericles sent only ten ships under Lacedaemonius, the son of Cimon. It looked as if he was trying to insult him, because Cimon's family was very well-disposed towards the Spartans. Pericles wanted to make sure that Lacedaemonius should have no major success as general and then stories would be spread around about his being pro-Spartan. Lacedaemonius did not even want to go on the expedition, but Pericles sent him off just the same – without a decent number of ships.

Athens later sent some more ships to Corcyra, but the fighting did not settle the issue. Both Corinth and Corcyra claimed that they had won the battle.

Thucydides I.55

In this way Corcyra survived the war with Corinth, and the Athenian ships left the island. But because Athens had fought against Sparta's ally Corinth when the peace treaty was still in force, Corinth now had her first reason for war against Athens.

Athens and Megara

Between them Thucydides and Plutarch give the following reasons for Athens' dispute with Megara:
1   The Megarians had taken land at Eleusis which was sacred to Demeter and Persephone and turned it into ordinary farm land for their own use.
2   They had taken in runaway slaves who had escaped from Athens.
3   They had put to death the Athenian messenger who had been sent to complain about what had been happening in Megara.

As a result the Athenians passed what is called the Megarian Decree. As well as denying the Megarians access to the Athenian Agora and all Athenian ports, it laid down that any Megarian found in Attica should be put to death and that Megara and the land round about should be invaded twice a year. The decree was in force by 432 B.C..

Plutarch *Pericles* 29

The Megarians complained to the Spartans that every agora and all harbours controlled by the Athenians were closed to them and that they had been driven away from their trade. 'Where is justice?' they cried. 'What of the oaths of peace and friendship we swore, Greek with Greek?'

The action against Megara was still going on in 425 B.C. and was by then one part of the full-scale war being fought against Sparta and her allies. In this year, a play by Aristophanes was produced in Athens. It was a satire about the effects of the war and drew attention to what was happening in Megara. In the following scene, an Athenian has made his own private peace and has set up a market for the Megarians.

Aristophanes *Acharnians* lines 750–63

ATHENIAN	Ah! A Megarian!
MEGARIAN	We've come to trade in this agora of yours.
ATHENIAN	How's it going then?
MEGARIAN	Well, we just sit by the fire and see who's shrunk the most.

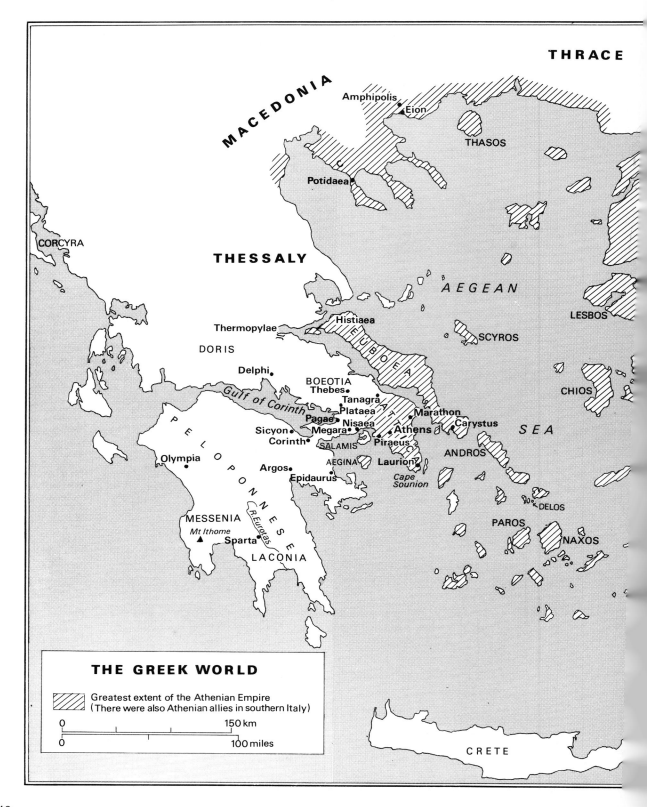

THRACE

MACEDONIA

Amphipolis
•Eion

THASOS

Potidaea

CORCYRA

THESSALY

AEGEAN

Thermopylae

Histiaea

DORIS

EUBOEA

SCYROS

LESBOS

Delphi•

BOEOTIA
Thebes•

Gulf of Corinth

Tanagra
Plataea

Pagae

CHIOS

Marathon

Sicyon•

Nisaea

Carystus

Megara•

Athens

SEA

Corinth•

SALAMIS

Piraeus

P
E
L
O
P
O
N
N
E
S
E

Olympia
•

Argos•

AEGINA

ANDROS

Laurion

Epidaurus

Cape
Sounion

•DELOS

MESSENIA

R.Eurotas

PAROS

Mt Ithome

Sparta

NAXOS

LACONIA

THE GREEK WORLD

Greatest extent of the Athenian Empire
(There were also Athenian allies in southern Italy)

| 0 | | 150 km |
| 0 | | 100 miles |

CRETE

BLACK SEA

Byzantium

PERSIAN

EMPIRE

LYDIA

ASIA

MOS IONIA

Mycale

Miletus

MINOR

R. Eurymedon

PAMPHYLIA

Halicarnassus

Phaselis

RHODES

CYPRUS

Cition

41

ATHENIAN	Drunk the most, did you say? Sounds all right – even better with a bit of music in the background! Everything else O.K.?
MEGARIAN	When I left to come here, the government was doing its best. I mean, there's no danger of a slow lingering end. They'll finish us off in a trice!
ATHENIAN	(*soothingly*) Never mind, it'll pass away soon.
MEGARIAN	*We* shall, that's for sure!
ATHENIAN	What else is going on at Megara? How's the price of corn?
MEGARIAN	Sky high! The gods would be lucky to get as much respect as a grain of corn.
ATHENIAN	Let's get down to business. Have you brought some salt to sell?
MEGARIAN	Isn't there enough in the sea? It is *your* sea, isn't it? Your navy seems to own it!
ATHENIAN	Well then, what about garlic?
MEGARIAN	What? You attack our land, dig up the plants like field-mice – and then you ask me about garlic!

VI.7   The Spartan ultimatum

Sparta listened to all the complaints from Corinth, Megara and other cities, and put their cases to Athens. They demanded that Athens should respect her allies' independence.

Thucydides I.139

The point which the Spartans spelt out most clearly was that there would not be a war if Athens would cancel the Megarian Decree. The Athenians would not give in over their allies, nor would they revoke the Decree.

In the end, representatives arrived from Sparta with an ultimatum. Instead of going over the same ground all over again, they gave this simple message: 'Sparta wants peace, and peace there would be, if you would only let the Greek cities manage their own affairs.'

VI.8   The Athenian reply

Thucydides I.139

The Athenians then met in the Assembly to hold a debate on the question. They resolved to look at all sides of the matter once and for all and then to give Sparta an answer. Lots of people came forward to speak, giving their views on both sides. 'We have to fight this war!' some said. 'Let's have done with the Megarian Decree,' said others. 'Why should it come between us and peace?' Among the speakers was Pericles.

The following extracts are from a long speech which Pericles made at this point, according to Thucydides. His account was not intended to be a word-for-word transcript of the actual speech, but a combination of arguments which are being put forward, memories of the speech, and ideas which fitted in with Pericles'

42

policy at the time. Thucydides probably also includes points about Athens' situation that he himself felt were relevant.

Thucydides
I.140–44

'No one should think that we would be going to war over some trivial matter, if we refused to revoke the Megarian Decree. The Spartans have pushed this issue to the front, and say that there needn't be a war if we revoke this decree. But this "trivial matter" is something that will show whether you are going to stand by your policy. If you give in, they will think that it is because you are afraid and they will immediately demand that you give way on a more important point. But by standing firm on this, you will show them that they have to deal with you on equal terms.'

Sparta, Pericles says, is good at fighting battles on land but has neither the money nor the organisation to fight a long war. Nor has she had the long experience of naval warfare that Athens has had.

'Sea-power is a huge advantage. Look at it like this: imagine we were living on an island. We'd be absolutely safe from attack, wouldn't we? Well, we're not on an island but we must pretend we are; we must leave our land and our houses and protect the sea and the city. We shall lose our land and our homes, and we shall be angry at the loss, but this must not lead us to fight a battle with the Spartans, because this is where they are better than we are. It is not the loss of houses or of land that should distress us but the loss of men's lives. Men come first: everything else is produced by them. What's more, if I thought I could persuade you to do it, I would tell you to go out and destroy your property yourselves and show the Spartans that you are not going to give in for the sake of your possessions.

'You will win in the end. The reasons I have given should make you confident of that, and there are many other reasons too, but you must be strong-minded: you must not try to bring any more cities under your control, and you must not go out looking for trouble.

'So what should we do now? Let us send the Spartans home with this answer: first, we shall let Megara into our Agora and our ports, but only if Sparta stops expelling foreign citizens, either ourselves or our allies (after all, under the treaty we are as free to issue the Megarian Decree as she is to drive out foreigners); second, we shall give our allies independence, if they were independent when we made the treaty (but at the same time the Spartans must also let their allies be independent and have whatever government they want, not the government that is useful to the Spartans); third, we will accept arbitration under the terms of the treaty; and finally, we shall not start a war but we shall defend ourselves against those who do.'

Thucydides
I.145

This was Pericles' speech. The Athenians thought that he had given the best advice and voted as he had told them to. They replied to the Spartans as he had suggested, listing the various conditions. They summed up the whole question saying, 'You cannot order us to do anything. Negotiation on equal terms is all we can consider. That was laid down in the treaty.'

The Spartans returned home and no more representatives were sent.

VII The second Peloponnesian War and the death of Pericles

VII.1 Preparations for war

Thucydides
II.7

Now the Athenians began to prepare for war, as did Sparta and her allies. Both sides planned to send representatives to the Persian king and to other foreign powers in the hope of getting their help. They also tried to make an ally of any city that was not already allied to either side.

The Spartans already had some ships, but they wanted to increase the number to 500. They therefore ordered each of their allies in Italy and Sicily to build a number of extra ships (the bigger the city, the more ships had to be provided), and also to contribute a sum of money.

The Athenians made sure of the allies they already had and sent out representatives, especially to places bordering on the Peloponnese. They did this because they realised that if they could build up a reliable friendship with these places, they could wear down the Spartans by fighting them on all sides.

Thucydides
II.10

Sparta instructed all her allies, both in the Peloponnese and outside, to raise an army and get ready everything that was needed for a foreign campaign. Their aim, they said, was to invade Attica. When each city had completed its preparations, they all gathered at the Isthmus of Corinth at the appointed time. Each state brought two-thirds of its total army.

431
B.C.

Thucydides
II.13

Pericles repeated the advice he had given the Athenians before. They were to prepare themselves for war and bring their property from the country into the city. They were not to go out and fight, but they were to come inside the city and defend it. Their strength lay in their fleet, so it must be well-equipped. The allies would need a firm hand since Athens relied on the money that the allies paid in tribute. To be successful in war, he said, good strategy and lots of money were both required.

Athens' financial position as outlined by Pericles:	
	Talents
Tribute from allies: average per annum	600
Silver (in coins) on the Acropolis*	6000
Miscellaneous: gold & silver offerings, sacred vessels, spoil from Persians	minimum 500

*Originally 9700. Some of this had been used for public buildings, including the Propylaea, and also for military purposes.

Athenian 2-obol coin.
406 B.C.

To this grand total, Pericles added treasures in other temples, which they could use. If they were absolutely desperate, there was the gold on the statue of Athene herself: there was, he explained, a weight of 40 talents of pure gold on the statue and it could all be removed. However, if they used this gold to preserve their own safety, they would have to put back afterwards at least as much as they had taken.

Pericles then lists the number of troops – infantry, guards, cavalry, archers – at their disposal, and mentions a fleet of 300 triremes ready to serve.

The move into the city

Thucydides II.14, 17
The Athenians took Pericles' advice. They brought in from the country their wives, children and all their household property. They even dismantled the woodwork on their houses. They sent their sheep and cattle over to Euboea and the islands nearby. However, the move was painful, because most of the people had been used to living in the country all their lives.

When they arrived in Athens, a few had houses of their own to go to or were able to lodge with friends or relatives. But most of them had to make their homes in the empty parts of the city in the temples and shrines of the heroes. They were kept strictly out of some other sacred land, including the Acropolis.

A lot of people settled in the towers along the walls. In fact, wherever there was a space there was someone living in it. When all the people flocked in together, they simply could not be fitted into the city; but later, they divided up most of Piraeus and the land between the Long Walls and settled there.

VII.2 Attica is invaded

The Spartan king, at the head of the Peloponnesian army, advanced on Attica very slowly. The troops were impatient, thinking that if they had proceeded more quickly they could have prevented the Athenians from taking themselves and their possessions into the safety of the city. But the king hoped at first that the Athenians would give in when they saw their land being ravaged. Later, he hoped that they would come out and fight a pitched battle.

Plutarch *Pericles* 33
The Peloponnesians advanced as far as Acharnae, ravaging the land as they went, and there they pitched camp. Acharnae is very close to Athens, and the Spartans thought that the Athenians would never put up with this: they would be so angry and their pride would be so hurt that they would fight against them. But Pericles thought that it would be a dreadful risk to join in battle with 60,000 hoplites from the Peloponnese and Boeotia: Athens herself would be at stake. He therefore tried to calm the people who were anxious to fight and were indignant at what was happening to their land. 'If you cut trees down,' he said, 'they'll soon grow; but if men are killed, it's not so easy to find more of them.'

Pressure to go out and fight grew steadily as the Athenians saw what was happening to their land so near to the city.

The Acharnians were especially keen that Athens should march out and fight. They felt that they were a large group in the state; and besides, it was their land that was being devastated. All in all, the city was thoroughly stirred up. The people were angry with Pericles and remembered none of his earlier advice. Instead, they blamed him for not leading them into a battle, though he was general, and believed that he was responsible for everything they were now suffering.

Pericles under attack

Pericles realised that the Athenians were aggrieved at what was happening at that time and were not thinking things out properly. On the other hand, he was sure that he was right in not wanting to go out and fight. He therefore refused to summon the people to the Assembly, as he was afraid that he would be persuaded to act against his better judgment. Instead, he shut up the city, protected it all round with guards and did what he thought best without taking any notice of the rowdy protests and grumbles. Even so, many of his friends begged and implored him, and many of his enemies threatened and accused him; he was the butt of rude songs and was ridiculed for being a cowardly general and letting the enemy have everything their own way.

VII.3   Athens attacks by sea

Pericles sent a fleet of 100 ships against the Peloponnese, but did not sail with it himself. Instead, he stayed behind to manage the city and keep everything under control until the Spartans and their allies withdrew. Even after they had gone, many people were suffering acutely from the war, so he won them over by handing out money and proposing to share out any land that they conquered. For instance, he drove out all the people of Aegina and divided the island among the Athenians by lot.

The people were also encouraged by what the enemy was suffering. The fleet that was sailing round the Peloponnese devastated much of the land and destroyed villages and small cities. This showed that although the enemy did the Athenians a lot of harm on land, at sea the Athenians could give as good as they got.

As well as their action at sea, the Athenians also invaded Megara, and devastated its territory as they had threatened in the Megarian Decree.

In the winter of this same year, the Athenians gave a public funeral for those who had been the first to die in the war. This was a tradition of theirs. Pericles was chosen to make the speech.

VII.4   The plague

Thucydides
II.47

As soon as summer began, the Spartans and their allies invaded Attica
again. As before, they brought two-thirds of their total fighting forces, and
as before, their commander was the Spartan king. They made themselves a
base, and ravaged the land.

430
B.C.

   The Spartans had not been in Attica for many days before the plague
broke out among the Athenians for the first time. It is said that it had
attacked other places before, but no one could remember it being so
widespread or so destructive anywhere else. To begin with, doctors could
not put a stop to it: they tried various remedies but had no understanding
of the disease. In fact, it was the doctors who died in greatest numbers
because they were in contact with the illness more than anyone else. No
other human skill was of any use, nor were prayers in temples, questions to
oracles or other similar things. In the end, people stopped believing in
them, as they were so overcome by the disaster.

> The historian Thucydides caught the plague himself and was one of the few to
> recover. He describes the disease and its effects in detail, but it has not been firmly
> identified with any disease known today. It seems to have affected the whole body,
> starting with the head and working through the chest and digestive system to the
> hands and feet.

Some symptoms

Thucydides
II.49–53

The skin was not all that hot to touch. It was flushed and angry-looking
rather than pale, and broke out in small blisters and sores. But inside, the
body burnt fiercely so that the patients could not bear the feel of even the
lightest muslin garment. They had to go naked and what they wanted most
of all was to throw themselves into cold water. In fact, many of those who
had no one to look after them actually did throw themselves into water-
tanks, driven by a thirst that they could not quench whether they drank
much or little. They could not keep still and were unable to sleep
throughout the illness.

   People who were generally fit and strong were no better off than the
weak: the plague overcame them all alike, however they were nursed.

The effects of the plague

The most terrible thing about the plague was the way people lost heart
when they realised they were going down with the disease. They gave up
hope and because of this they let themselves go, instead of holding out
against the disease.

   The disease spread from person to person as people cared for each other;
that was the biggest cause of death. People just died like sheep.
Consequently, some people were afraid to visit the sick, so that they died
alone; in many houses, not one person remained alive, because there had
been no one to care for them. But other people did visit the sick and died as

a result. These were mostly the people with some sense of conscience. They were ashamed to put themselves first, and so they went to their friends, at times when even the relatives were so overcome by the burden of the disaster that they had stopped lamenting over the dead.

This was not the only way in which the plague gave rise to a new kind of lawlessness in the city. People were not held back by a fear of the gods. 'What difference does it make,' they asked themselves, 'whether I respect the gods or not? Everyone is dying just the same.' Nor did the laws have much effect: people did not expect to live long enough to be tried and punished for their wrongdoings. In fact, it seemed instead that they had already been sentenced to death and that they might as well get some enjoyment out of life before the sentence was carried out.

VII.5   Anger with Pericles

Plutarch
Pericles 34

The plague had a bad effect not only on their bodies but on their minds as well. They were furious with Pericles and tried to bring him down, just as a man who is out of his mind will attack his doctor or his father. They were encouraged in this by his enemies. The plague, they insisted, had been caused by crowding the country people into the city. Here, in the summer, large numbers were packed into shanty-towns of makeshift, airless dwellings, where they had to stay indoors without exercise, instead of being out in the fresh air as they had been used to before. 'This is Pericles' fault!' they declared. 'War breaks out, so he brings all the country people flooding within the walls. He then leaves them, without anything to do, shut up like cattle, with no change in their condition and no relief. No wonder they spread the disease from one to another!'

Thucydides
II.55

Meanwhile the Peloponnesians had devastated the plain of Attica and moved on as far as Laurion where the Athenian silver-mines are. First they devastated the part that faces the Peloponnese, and then the other part that faces Euboea and Andros.

Plutarch
Pericles 35

Pericles wanted to remedy the city's problems and harm the enemy at the same time. So he manned 150 triremes and put a large force of the best infantry and horsemen on board. He set sail and besieged the sacred city of Epidaurus. There were high hopes that it would be taken. However, an outbreak of the plague put a stop to his plans by claiming not only his own men but also those who had anything to do with them.

The strain of fighting the war, suffering from the plague and seeing their land devastated twice made the Athenians turn against Pericles' whole policy of war with the Spartans. They tried to make peace with Sparta but without success. They were now overcome with anger and despair.

Thucydides
II.65

Pericles made a speech to the people, and tried in this way to turn the Athenians' anger away from himself, and to take their minds off their

Reconstruction of a house built in the Attic countryside about 421 B.C. (There are very few remains of houses from this period.)

present sufferings. As far as public affairs were concerned, they were convinced by his advice: they did not send any more representatives to Sparta and applied themselves to the war more vigorously. But as individuals, they still felt aggrieved at all the things that had gone wrong. The people had not had many possessions to start with and had been deprived even of those, while the well-to-do had lost their fine properties in the country together with their houses and expensive furniture. Worst of all, there was war instead of peace. They did not stop feeling angry with Pericles until they had made him pay a fine. But crowds are always changing their minds, and it was not long before they elected him general again and put him in charge of everything.

429
B.C.

VII.6   The death of Pericles

Although Pericles had become popular with the people again, his private life was far from happy. The plague had deprived him of many friends and relatives, including both his legitimate sons. According to the citizenship law that Pericles himself had introduced in 451, no one was allowed Athenian citizenship unless both his parents had been Athenian citizens. This meant that Pericles' only surviving son was excluded from citizenship, because he was the illegitimate son of Pericles and Aspasia.

Plutarch
Pericles 37
Pericles now asked that the law he himself had introduced about illegitimate children might be waived in his case. He made this request so that his name and family would not die out now that he had no legitimate heir. It was very strange that the law which had been enforced so strictly against so many should be waived for the benefit of the very man who had introduced it. But the tragedy that Pericles had suffered in his private life seemed like a punishment for looking down on other people and thinking so much of himself. The Athenians' hearts were softened, and so they let him enter his illegitimate son in the family lists and give him his own name.

Plutarch
Pericles 38
Then Pericles seems to have caught the plague. There was no sudden onset or acute illness such as other people had suffered, but a sort of weakness that lingered on, producing different symptoms. His body slowly wasted away and his mind and spirit lost their strength.

Thucydides
II.65
When he died, the war had been going on for two years and six months.

429
B.C.

Plutarch
Pericles 39
As the war proceeded, the Athenians immediately began to value Pericles and he was sadly missed. While he was alive, some people were weighed down by a sense of his power, as if it kept them hidden away from public life. But after his death, they saw what other orators and leaders of the people were like, and had to admit that Pericles had been unique: he had been dignified, but not arrogant, and he had commanded respect while still being gentle in his manner.

Epilogue

The war between Athens and Sparta continued, with a brief period of peace between 421 and 415 B.C. There were successes and failures on both sides, and the Athenians were weakened by a disastrous campaign against Sicily, in which they lost a fleet. Athens fought on, but was defeated by Sparta in 404 B.C.

In 411 B.C. Athens' democracy was overthrown and there was a harsh government, known as the Thirty Tyrants, in control until 403 B.C. But after this, Athens' democracy was restored, and in the fourth century she regained some of her power. She also continued to flourish as a centre of literature, art and philosophy.

Even if we give in at some time (and it is the nature of all things to grow weaker), yet further generations will still remember us for this: no Greeks ruled over more Greeks then we did; we stood firm in the mightiest of wars, whether states fought against us on their own or whether they joined forces with each other; and we lived in a city that in every respect reached a pinnacle of prosperity and magnificence.   Thucydides II.64

1 The Spartans

The town of Sparta is situated in the Peloponnese along the fertile valley of the river Eurotas. The surrounding area is mountainous and the sea is 45 kms (28 miles) away. Unlike other Greek towns, Sparta had no city walls. Not much is known of the early history of Sparta, but by 700 B.C. she had conquered most of Laconia and neighbouring Messenia. Messenia provided her with much-needed agricultural land; the Messenians were enslaved and farmed the land for the Spartans.

Sparta developed quite differently from other Greek states, both in her government and the way her society was organised. It is not easy to know what Sparta was actually like. The Spartans wrote very little about themselves, and other Greeks, although intrigued by the Spartan system, did not always base what they wrote on first-hand experience.

Life in Sparta

The Spartans believed that a man called Lycurgus was responsible for their laws and traditions.

Spartans were not allowed to bring their sons up as they pleased. Lycurgus ordered that all boys at the age of seven were to be taken away from their family and put in 'companies' where they would be brought up and looked after together. They learnt only the bare essentials of reading and writing.

Inside of a Spartan cup painted with warriors.

The rest of their education was designed to make them obey commands, endure hardships and win battles.

A youth of 20 is in charge of each company of boys. He supervises their mock battles and makes them serve him at meals indoors. He gives the bigger boys the job of fetching wood and the smaller ones have to go out to collect the herbs. They steal what they fetch, and anyone who is caught is given several lashes of the whip – for being a careless and unskilful thief. They also steal whatever food they can, and learn how to be clever at setting upon people who are asleep or off their guard.   Plutarch *Lycurgus* 16–17

There is a story that one boy had stolen a fox and was carrying it hidden under his cloak. He allowed the animal to tear out his bowels with its teeth and claws rather than let his theft be detected.   Plutarch *Lycurgus* 18

Girls in Sparta, unlike girls in other Greek states, were given some athletic training, including running and wrestling.

Lycurgus gave every father authority over other men's children as well as his own. If a boy tells his own father that he has been whipped by one of the other fathers, it is a disgrace if the parent does not give his son another whipping.

He also made it permissible for one man to use another man's servants if the need arose. He also made hunting dogs common property. Those who needed them would invite the owner to hunt and, if he was busy, he would send his dogs along. They use horses in the same way. So if someone is ill or needs a carriage, or wants to get somewhere quickly, he takes any horse he finds, uses it carefully and then returns it.

Xenophon *Spartan Constitution* 6

A Spartan cup of about 550 B.C. (Painted pottery did not develop in Sparta after this.)

52

The following story tells of an occasion, about 100 years after the Persian Wars, when Sparta's allies complained that the Spartans had only fielded a few soldiers for battle. (Agesilaus was king of Sparta from 399–360 B.C.)

Agesilaus ordered all the allies to sit down with each other in one big group, and the Spartans to sit apart by themselves. Then his herald ordered all the potters to stand up first of all. When they had all stood up, the herald gave the same orders to the blacksmiths, and the carpenters and builders, and so on through all the craftsmen. Before long almost all the allies had stood up, but not a single Spartan – for they are not allowed to do manual work or to learn about it. Then Agesilaus laughed and said, 'So, men, you see how many more soldiers we have sent out to battle than you.'

Plutarch *Agesilaus* 26

Society

We know Spartan society was divided into three classes, although it is unclear how this came about.
1   *The Equals*. This was the name given to full Spartan citizens.
2   *The Perioikoi* (meaning 'people who live round about'). These were the neighbouring people. They were citizens of their own independent communities, but could be called upon to fight for the Spartans without any say in the decision to go to war. Most of the Perioikoi were peasant farmers.
3   *The Helots*. These were like serfs in that they had no political rights and no freedom of movement. They worked the land for the Spartan citizens, but were owned by the state rather than by individuals. Sparta took half their produce as rent, leaving them only the remainder to live on. (It is not known whether the Spartans had slaves as well as helots.) Each Spartan soldier was attended by a helot, and sometimes the helots fought in battle too.

Aristotle tells us that when the officials took up office they made a formal declaration of war on the helots. The purpose of this was to make sure that killing them was no offence.   Plutarch *Lycurgus* 28

The Equals claimed to have come originally from Doris in central Greece, the origins of the perioikoi are uncertain, and the helots were almost certainly descendants of the original native inhabitants of the area.

Government

The Spartan system of government, like many other things in Sparta, was quite different from that of other Greek cities.
    There was an *Assembly* at which all *Equals* over the age of 30 could vote on decisions about war and peace, foreign policy and new laws. However the Assembly could not put forward proposals of its own but could only vote on

proposals made by the *Council of Elders*. This consisted of 28 life members over the age of 60 and Sparta's two *kings*.

Finance, law and order, and education were in the hands of the five *Ephors* ('overseers'). They had considerable power but held office for only one year and could not be re-elected.

Sparta and Athens compared

Imagine that Sparta were to become a deserted city, with only the temples and foundations of buildings remaining. I think that after some time people in the future would find it very hard to believe that the town had really had as much power as they had been told. The Spartans occupy two-fifths of the Peloponnese and are the leaders not only of the whole Peloponnese but also of many allies outside the Peloponnese. Yet Sparta would not look as important as you would expect, because the place is not laid out in a regular pattern and there are no grand temples or monuments; it is just a group of villages, like towns were in the olden days. On the other hand, the opposite is true of Athens: if Athens were to be deserted, you would guess from the appearance of the remains that the city had been twice as powerful as it actually is.   Thucydides I.10

Modern Sparta with the Taygetos mountains in the distance. There are virtually no remains in Sparta from the fifth century B.C.

2 Athens and her fleet

Piraeus

The photograph below shows an aerial view of Athens' port, Piraeus (modern Pireefs), looking north west. The names of the three harbours, from north to south, are Cantharos, Zea and Munychia.

Cantharos was, and still is, the main harbour. At Zea there were sheds for 196 triremes (warships) arranged like the spokes of a giant wheel. Another 82 triremes could be berthed at Munychia, which is today a yachting harbour.

Themistocles' development of Piraeus was continued by Pericles. The street plan designed for him can still be seen in the layout of the modern roads.

After the harbours at Piraeus had been built, the Athenians no longer had to pull their ships up onto the beach as they had done at Phaleron.

The fleet of triremes

A major development in the growth of Athens' fleet came during the period between the two Persian invasions.

The revenue from the mines at Laurion had brought great wealth to the Athenian treasury, and the Athenians were going to share it out by giving each citizen ten drachmas. Themistocles persuaded them not to divide up the money in this way, but instead to build a fleet of 200 ships for the war they were fighting against the island of Aegina. (It was the outbreak of this war which saved Greece, because it made seamen of the Athenians.) In fact the ships were not used for their original purpose, but this was how they came to be available to Greece in her hour of need.

Herodotus Histories VII.144

The Athenians were not the only people to use the trireme, but they were the only ones who developed and improved it. The trireme is frequently mentioned by ancient writers and it is especially famous for its part in the battle of Salamis. It seems to have been a ship which could move quickly in battle and with great effect, but unfortunately no detailed description or complete picture of it has come down to us. There have been many ideas about what it was like and the question was fiercely debated in the longest ever series of letters in *The Times* newspaper. Scholars argued about such problems as the size of the stucture of the hull and the number and arrangement of the crew.

A full-size working trireme has now been built as a result of years of research by John Coates, a naval architect, and John Morrison, a classical scholar. They pieced together fragments of archaeological evidence and clues from ancient writers and tested their findings against the theory and practice of ship-building. The *Olympias*, financed and built by the Greek navy, put to sea for the first time in 1987, and trials and further study have revealed a great deal about how this type of ship worked.

Here are some examples of the different kinds of evidence used by Coates and Morrison.

The *Olympias*

Archaeological evidence

Size

In 1886 a report was published of the excavations of the sheds at Zea. The maximum dry length of a shed was 37 metres. They were separated from each other by rows of pillars, and the clear width between these was 6 metres.

The crew

More information comes from the 'Naval Inventories'. These lists of ships and gear were discovered in Piraeus, inscribed on stone slabs. Amongst other things, they list the numbers of oars per ship (170, plus spares), the oarsmen in each category, the condition of the leather 'sleeves' for the lowest row of oars, and the number of sails (2).

From these and other sources, we can calculate that the crew of a trireme consisted of 200 men, divided as follows:

170 rowers
1 helmsman and gang of 5 to work mainsail
2 bow officers and gang of 5 to work forwardsail
1 boatswain, 1 purser (in charge of expenditure), 1 shipwright, 1 piper
10 hoplites on deck, 4 archers.

This ram was discovered near Haifa. It is too heavy for a trireme, but gives archaeologists a good indication of shape and structure, since it was found with the timbers still attached.

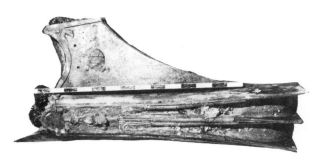

This fragment of Attic pottery shows oars on a warship. It was painted in the sixth century B.C. but is useful evidence for the fifth-century trireme as well.

There is no archaeological evidence for what the whole ship was like. Wrecks of Greek cargo ships have been discovered, but no wreck of a trireme has ever come to light. (Modern calculations indicate that a rammed trireme would be sufficiently buoyant to stay afloat. The author Xenophon (*History of Greece* 1.7.32) tells us of a general who escapes on a ship which had been 'sunk'.) The problem is made more difficult because no picture exists showing a complete trireme.

Evidence from ancient writers

The word trireme comes from the words for 'three' and 'oars'.

The oars and hull of the *Olympias*

The rowers

The comic playwright Aristophanes makes it clear that some rowers were seated above the others with some rude remarks about what might happen to a rower in the lower level beneath someone else's backside.

The 'Lenormant' relief. This was carved in about 410 B.C. and is named after the person who discovered it. Details may originally have been painted. The carving is not very well preserved.

Some information is also given by Thucydides, who tells us of a surprise attack which the Peloponnesians planned to make in the early years of the war against Athens (429 B.C.).

The plan was that each sailor should take his oar, his cushion and his oarloop, and go overland from Corinth to the sea on the Athenian side. They were then to reach Megara as quickly as possible, launch 40 ships which happened to be in the docks and immediately sail to Piraeus.

Thucydides II.93

The trireme in action

This passage gives some idea of how triremes operated on voyages and in battle. The Athenian general Iphicrates was short of time on this campaign, so he turned the voyage itself into a series of training exercises.

When Iphicrates started to sail round the Peloponnese, he took with him everything he needed to fight a battle at sea. He left his large sails behind as though he were sailing into battle, and hardly used his small sails either, even when there was a favourable wind. Because the men were made to row instead, they grew fitter and the ships travelled faster.

When it was time for the morning and evening meal, he would give a signal and make the ships race for the shore. Again, if they were having a meal on enemy land, he set look-outs on the land as usual, but he also raised the ships' masts and had men watching from the top of them. They could see much further from this viewpoint than they could have done on the ground. While they were voyaging by day, he trained them to form lines when he gave the signal, either ahead of each other or side by side. As a result, they had practised and become skilled at the manoeuvres necessary for fighting a sea battle before they reached that part of the sea which they thought was controlled by the enemy.

Xenophon, *History of Greece* 6.2.22–30

Sometimes the number of soldiers on deck could be increased, but this could cause problems. When fighting against Sparta, the Athenian fleet once found itself forced to fight in unusual circumstances, described by the Spartan general.

'The Athenians have many hoplites on deck, which is not their usual practice. They also have many javelin men on board, Acarnanians and others. They are landsmen, so to speak, and will not have learnt how to throw their javelins from a sitting position. This will surely put their ships at risk and they will all be in confusion because they are not used to movement of this sort.'

Thucydides VII.67

How fast was a trireme?

From	To	Distance	Time	(Source)
Byzantium	Heraclea	236 km (129 sea miles)	16–18 hours	(Xenophon)
Arginusae	Rhoeteum	229 km (124 sea miles)	16–18 hours	(Thucydides)

Both these journeys are mentioned as unusual feats.

3 Democracy at Athens

The word 'democracy' comes from the ancient Greek words *demos* meaning 'people' and *kratos* meaning 'power'.

I cannot praise the constitution the Athenians have chosen because they make the ordinary people better off than the wealthy upper classes. But this is what they think best, and I will show how well they maintain this system.

   The first thing I want to say is that at Athens it is right for the poor and the people in general to have more power than the wealthy and the high-born. This is my reason: it is the people who row the ships and give the city its power. Just think of the steersmen, the time-keepers, the unit commanders, the look-outs and the people who build the ships; these are the ones who give power to the city much more than the hoplites, the high-born and the better sort of people.

   This being the case, it seems right that everyone should have a share in government positions, both those chosen by lot and those chosen by election, and that everyone should be able to speak his mind.

Old Oligarch 1 and 2 (extracts)

The Athenian democracy had several parts: the Assembly consisting of all the citizens, the jury courts, the Council of Five Hundred and the Council of the Areopagus. There were also the leading officials: the archons and the generals. Together these bodies and officials were responsible for the business of the state: finance, making laws, religious affairs, running the courts, organising elections and relations with other states.

   The way in which the state was run developed over a long period of time. During that time some elements of the democracy gained more power and others lost some of their power.

a) Citizenship and the Assembly

Under the Athenian democracy decisions were made by all the citizens, meeting in the Assembly.

Citizenship

To be a citizen, an Athenian had to be male, freeborn and native to the city. Women, slaves and foreigners had no say in the democracy.

The simplest definition of a citizen is 'one who shares in government and the administration of justice'.   Aristotle *Politics* 1275a

   In the archonship of Antidotos [451 B.C.], owing to the large number of citizens, they passed a proposal made by Pericles that a man could only be a citizen if both his parents were of citizen birth.

Aristotle *Constitution of Athens* 26

The Assembly

Democracy at Athens developed as the power of the Assembly increased over the years.

In this passage Socrates is urging a young man not to feel shy about speaking in the Assembly. His argument indicates the range of people who attended the Assembly.

'You are not shy with extremely clever people. Nor are you nervous of people who have a great deal of influence. And yet you don't have the guts to speak in front of those who are the least clever and have no influence. Surely you aren't too shy to meet cleaners and dyers, shoemakers, carpenters, farmers, merchants, market people? Well, these are the sort of people who make up the Assembly.' Xenophon *Memoirs* 3.7

According to Aristotle, the Assembly met forty times a year. We do not possess a proper account of any of its meetings, but some of the details can be worked out from Aristophanes' plays. The extract below comes from the beginning of *The Acharnians* which won first prize in the early years of the war with Sparta.

MR JUST (Dikaiopolis)
I haven't felt so sore since I was first old enough to wash myself and got all the soap in my eyes. They've fixed a business meeting for the Assembly at sunrise, and here's the Pnyx Hill – deserted. They're all chatting in the Agora, and wandering up and down to avoid the rope with the red paint on it. Not even the Council committee are here; they'll arrive late, and when they do get here you can't imagine how they'll push and shove to get the front bench – hordes of them all rushing down together. But as far as peace is concerned, they couldn't give a damn. My poor old city!

So here I am, absolutely ready to shout and interrupt and hurl insults at the speakers if anyone talks about anything except peace. Ah, here are the Councillors, now it's midday. Didn't I tell you? It's just like I said – everyone pushing and shoving for a place at the front.

HERALD
Move forward! Move and get inside the purified area. Who wishes to address the people? Aristophanes *The Acharnians* lines 17–27, 37–44

b) The Council of Five Hundred

The Council is selected by lot and consists of 500 members, fifty from each tribe. Each of the tribes takes its turn at being the Council committee. Those who belong to the committee first dine together in the Tholos. (They receive money from the state for this purpose.) Then they summon the Council and the Assembly of the people. They select a chairman by lot,

The ruins of the Agora compared with a reconstruction showing how the buildings looked at the end of the fifth century.

W B DINSMOOR, JR.-1981

and he holds the position for one day and one night. He has to stay in the Tholos and choose one third of the committee to stay with him.

Aristotle Constitution of Athens *43–4*

The Council passes judgment on most of the government officials, especially those who handle public funds. Private individuals can lay information against any of the officials they wish and accuse them of not acting in accordance with the law. If the Council passes a verdict of guilty, then these officials also have the right to appeal to the jury court.

The Council, then, does not have supreme power, but it does discuss beforehand everything that is brought before the people. The people cannot vote on anything which has not been previously discussed by the Council and put on the agenda by the committee.

Aristotle Constitution of Athens *43–5*

Archaeological evidence

'Tholos' is the Greek word for a circular building. The one in the Agora is dated by pottery to around 470–60 B.C. and is 18.33 metres in diameter. Some

The centre of Athens at the end of the fifth century.

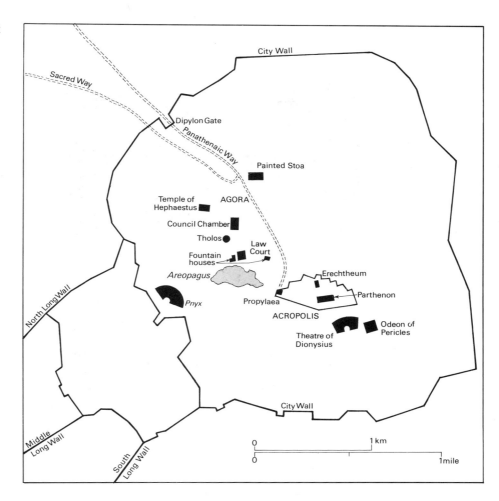

Fragments of pottery found near the Tholos.

fragments of the crockery used at the committee meals have been discovered nearby. The pieces come from simple black-glazed cups, bowls and pitchers. On some of them is scratched ΔE – the first two letters of the Greek word *demosion*, meaning 'public property' or 'owned by the *demos* (people)'. The Tholos was built over the ruins of a large private house, which may have belonged to the tyrant Peisistratos.

Next to the Tholos was the Council Chamber. The ruins of this are very scant, but archaeologists think it was built around 500 B.C. If each seat was half a metre wide, the main room could seat 500 people around three of its sides.

c) The archons

In ancient times the archons, who ruled the city, were chosen from the noble and the wealthy. At first they held office for life, but later [c.750 B.C.] this was changed to ten years.   Aristotle *Constitution of Athens* 3

The man chosen to be chief archon gave his name to the year, and if Athenians wanted to give a date, they would say 'In the archonship of . . .'. Lists of these archons were inscribed on stone and still survive.

In the time of Solon [594 B.C.] the archons had the power to give final judgment in lawsuits, and not, as now, just to hold a preliminary hearing.

Aristotle Constitution of Athens 3

Although they originally came only from the wealthy families, the archons were actually chosen by a vote of the people. People such as Solon, Cleisthenes and Themistocles had all been archons. However, a change was made in this system in the period between the two Persian Wars.

In the archonship of Telesinus [487/6 B.C.], they selected the nine archons by lot, tribe by tribe, out of 500 who had been previously selected by the men of each district. Aristotle Constitution of Athens 22

In addition to legal matters, the archons were also responsible for several religious events and for appointing wealthy citizens to pay for dramatic productions.

d) The council of the Areopagus

[In the time of Solon] the council of the Aeropagus was responsible for keeping watch over the laws, but in fact it controlled most of the important

The Areopagus (Ares' Hill) with the Acropolis in the background and Mt Hymettos in the distance.

affairs of the city, with supreme power to punish offenders and impose fines. This was because the members of the Areopagus were chosen from the archons, and the archons were chosen from wealthy and important families.

Aristotle Constitution of Athens 3

The council of the Areopagus had a good reputation at the time of the Persian Wars and was said to have kept the Athenian constitution 'tightly tuned'.

Aristotle Politics 1304a 25

One effect of the new system of choosing archons by lot was a very gradual change in the council of the Areopagus. As time went by, it came to contain more and more people who had been selected by lot rather than by direct vote.

After the changes of 462 B.C. (see p.26), the Areopagus was left with only its function as a court for cases of homicide, wounding and arson.

e) The jury courts

In the early days, the archons and the council of the Areopagus seem to have had supreme power in legal matters. However, in Solon's time there was also a people's court where any citizen could appeal against a verdict he considered unjust. This court was originally a gathering of all the citizens, but later on jurors were chosen each year to be representatives of their fellow-citizens. This system of jury service, common in modern democracies, first began in Athens.

They say that the thing which gave most power to the masses was the right to appeal to a jury court.

Aristotle Constitution of Athens 9

Pericles was the first to introduce pay for the people who served in the jury courts. This was an attempt to make himself popular and counteract the wealth of Cimon. Some people criticise Pericles and say that the courts now began to deteriorate because it was the common people rather than the respectable ones who were keen to draw lots for the duty. Moreover, it was after this that bribery of juries began.

Aristotle Constitution of Athens 27

The pay for jury service was two obols; this was later raised to three. Some citizens could earn more than this in other jobs, so a part of the juries tended to be made up of those who were too old for work. The Athenians got a reputation for eagerness to serve on the juries. This was the subject of one of Aristophanes' plays, *The Wasps*, which was produced in 422 B.C.

BOY	Will you give me something, father, if I ask you?
FATHER	Of course, son. Tell me, what nice thing do you want me to buy? I suppose you'd like me to buy you some knucklebones to play with.
BOY	No. It's some figs I'd like. They're much sweeter.
FATHER	Hang me if I will!
BOY	Then I won't come any further with you.
FATHER	Look, out of this miserable jury-pay I've got to get a meal, firewood and meat for three of us – and you want figs!

BOY   Father, if the archon says the court won't sit today, where are
         we going to get lunch from? Is there any hope at all . . . ?
FATHER   *(Sighs)* I really don't know where our next meal will come from.
                                                        Aristophanes *Wasps* 291ff.

Aristotle, talking about the beginning of the Delian League, says that
contributions from the allies helped to pay for 6000 of these jurymen.

For most cases, the jurors were divided up into panels. The only information we
have about this in the fifth century is a speech which mentions a jury of 700
members. There is much more information about the fourth century, and 501
seems to have been the standard number then. Sometimes two or three panels of
jurymen were combined.

Unlike modern juries, these panels had to give their verdict by voting
immediately. There was no summing up from a judge, and no time to consider
their verdict.

f) The generals

We do not hear about generals before the time of Cleisthenes (507 B.C.), and they
are probably linked to his reorganisation of the Athenians into ten new tribes.
Originally, there was one general from each tribe, but later they were chosen from
all the citizens together.

In earlier times, all the famous leaders of the people had been archons, but by
the time of Cimon and Pericles the situation had changed, and leaders of the
people became generals instead. Although the archons retained some of the ancient
legal and religious duties, the generals took over as supreme army commanders. It
was also their responsibility to appoint wealthy citizens to maintain a trireme each
for a year.

There are some government positions which can bring either security or
danger to the whole people, depending on the quality of the man who holds
it. The people do not claim a share in these positions. They do not think
that they should have a share in the generalships or cavalry commands by
the drawing of lots. The people realise that there is more to be gained if
they do not hold these positions, but allow them to be held by the most
powerful men.   *Old Oligarch* 3 (extracts)

Every month there is a vote to see whether the generals seem to be doing
their duties properly. If the vote goes against any of them, he is put on trial
in the court. If he is convicted, the people decide what the penalty or fine is
to be; but if he is acquitted he takes up his duties again. On active service
the generals have the power to punish any breach of discipline with
imprisonment, dismissal or a fine – though a fine is not usual.
                                          Aristotle *Constitution of Athens* 61

4 Ostracism

ostracise: to exclude; to refuse to associate with someone.

The modern word 'ostracise' has a more general meaning than it had when it was first used in ancient Greece. In the 5th century B.C. ostracism meant a form of banishment. The word originally comes from the Greek word *ostrakon* which means a broken piece of pottery.

To give a general outline, the procedure was as follows. Each man took an ostrakon and wrote on it the name of the citizen he wished to be removed from the city. He then took it to a place in the Agora which was marked off with a wooden railing. The archons first counted the total number of the votes cast. (If there were fewer than 6,000 voters then the ostracism was void.) Then they separated the names and the man whose name had been written by the most people was proclaimed an exile for ten years, though he was allowed to receive the income from his property.

Plutarch *Aristeides* 7

The Athenians were not the only people to have ostracism; the people of Argos, Miletus and Megara also did. Nearly all the most accomplished men were ostracised: Aristeides, Cimon, Themistocles, Thucydides.

Ancient commentary on Aristophanes *Knights* line 855

Plutarch tells us how Aristeides was present at an ostracism when an illiterate man gave him an ostrakon and asked him to write the name 'Aristeides' on it. Aristeides was astonished and asked the man what he had against Aristeides. 'Nothing at all,' he replied, 'I'm just sick of hearing everyone calling him "the just".' Aristeides wrote down his name and gave back the ostrakon without saying anything.

Archaeological evidence

Over 1,000 ostraka have been found in the Agora and several thousand have been found nearby. One group of 190 ostraka was found to the south-east of the Agora. Each one was inscribed with the name of Themistocles – but handwriting experts have shown that they were only written by 14 different people. This was an unusual find; most ostraka were written by individual voters.

Ostraka

5 The Acropolis

The picture below shows how the Acropolis probably looked at the end of Pericles' building programme. The four numbered buildings are the ones which are best preserved today:

1. The Parthenon
2. The Propylaea (gateway)
3. The temple of Athene Nike (Athene the Victor)
4. The Erechtheum.

There were earlier temples to Athene on the Acropolis. The ruins of one are marked (A) on the picture and can still be seen. The ruins of another lie underneath the Parthenon. These belong to a temple that was still unfinished when it was destroyed by the Persians. Some of the column drums from this temple were used in the north wall of the Acropolis.

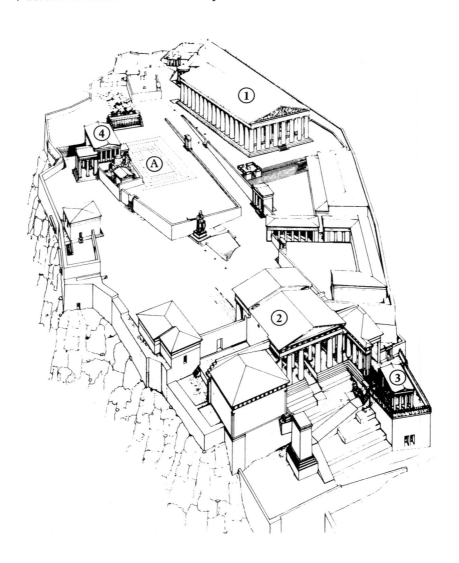

The Acropolis as it looked at the end of the building programme.

The building programme

B.C.
450	5,000 talents transferred to treasury of Athene to finance building
477	First building account of Parthenon
438	Dedication of Athene's statue in the Parthenon
437	First building account of Propylaea
433	Last building account of Propylaea
429	Death of Pericles
?425	Work begins on temple of Athene Nike
?421	Work begins on Erechtheum
490	First Persian invasion
480	Second Persian invasion
454	Delian League treasury moved to Athens

Some of the building accounts still survive. This one from the year 434/3 B.C. is for the Parthenon. It shows the receipt of 25,000 drachmas from the treasurers, 1,372 from the sale of gold and 1,354 from the sale of ivory. (The last two had been sold off as surplus to requirements.)

The Parthenon

The Parthenon is one of the world's most famous buildings. It is admired for its proportions and refinements in its design, as well as for its fine sculpture.

Proportion

Some Greeks felt that 'beauty' could be expressed in numbers. Works of art, they felt, should have a clear number of parts, and all the parts should be related to each other. It may have been the philosopher Pythagoras who first led people to think this way, about 100 years before the Parthenon was built.

The following diagrams show how the proportion of 9:4 was used throughout the Parthenon.

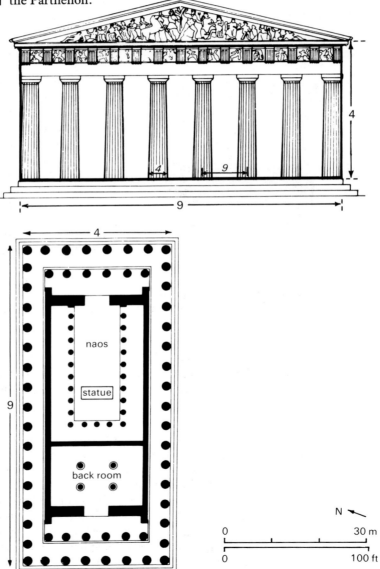

Refinements

The Parthenon seems to be made up of basic mathematical shapes, but it is not as simple as it seems.

1 At first sight, all the lines in the Parthenon seem to be straight. But if we look closely at the picture of the steps, we can see that they curve inwards and upwards towards the centre. The same curve is repeated along the architrave, the band of stone running across the top of the columns.

2 Careful measurements show that the corner columns are wider than the inner ones.

3 The columns also all lean inwards. If the corner columns were extended upwards, they would eventually meet over the centre point of the building.

These variations are usually called 'refinements'.

Why were they made? We know they were no accident, because we can measure the same effects on other temples. In any case, the stone is cut so accurately and the plan worked out so carefully, that an 'accident' of this sort seems impossible. In fact, it would be easier to build a temple without all these refinements.

Some theories are as follows:

a) Ictinus, the architect of the Parthenon, wrote a book on architecture. Although this does not survive, the Roman architect Vitruvius did have a copy of it and was perhaps influenced by it. He says that our eyes can be deceived.

If the temple platform is laid out level, it will appear to our eyes to be hollowed out. The corner columns are viewed against a background of just the open air, and therefore seem to be more slender than they actually are.

Vitruvius III c III

b) Another theory says that the purpose of all these refinements is to give 'life' to the building. Our minds want to see perfect rectangles and perfect straight lines, but our eyes keep noticing small variations. In this way the building keeps us fascinated in a sort of tension between what is real and what is imaginary. (Some even say that the bulge in the lower part of the columns is like a constantly flexed muscle on a giant arm.) A simpler version of this theory is that the refinements stop the building being too regular and dull.

c) A third theory says that the whole emphasis is on height and grandeur. The upward curve and the inward lean constantly make our eyes travel upwards.

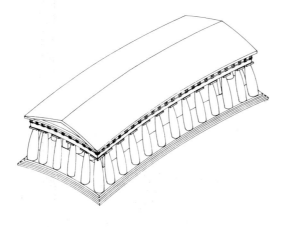

Even the bulge in the lower part of the columns is intended to send our eyes shooting to the top.

d) Perhaps the simplest theory of all is that the curves are there to ensure that the rainwater drains off properly.

The picture shows an exaggerated version of the refinements.

The sculpture

The pediments

The pediments are triangular gables at each end of the roof.

As you go into the temple called the Parthenon you will see sculptures on the parts they called the pediments. Those on the front depict the miraculous birth of Athene and those on the rear depict the contest for the land of Attica between Athene and Poseidon.   Pausanias 1.24.5

Athene was born from the head of Zeus. She won the contest for the land by presenting Attica with its first olive tree which was judged more useful than the salt water spring which Poseidon created. Much of the sculpture has now

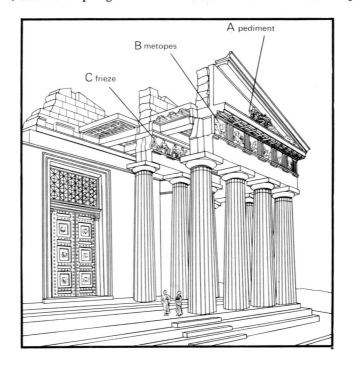

disappeared, but the three goddesses in the picture still survive from the east (front) pediment of the Parthenon.

The metopes

These are the small carved panels (1.3 metres square) that form part of the frieze on the outside of the temple, just below the pediments. Some of them show the story of how a Greek tribe called the Lapiths defeated the Centaurs, monsters who were half man and half horse. To the Greeks, this story represented the triumph of civilisation over barbarism. The other metopes show similar stories.

A metope which still remains on the Parthenon.

The frieze

The Parthenon had a second frieze, which ran around the outside of the sanctuary wall. It was placed high up and could be viewed between the tops of the columns. Along it is depicted a great procession of chariots and horses. There are also musicians, people carrying trays and pitchers, and animals being brought for sacrifice. Every four years, a great procession such as this moved through the streets of Athens to bring a new robe for the statue of Athene.

Since temples built at this time do not usually have pictures of ordinary human beings, this procession is thought to be something rather more special. The total number of men in the procession, not counting the charioteers, is 192 – exactly the number of men who are said to have died in the battle of Marathon. One theory, therefore, is that we are watching a procession of young men going to join the gods in eternal fame. This would explain why the gods in the central panel of the frieze are not watching the handing over of the robe, but are looking towards the procession.

The central panel of the frieze.

Most of the frieze, and several other pieces of sculpture, were removed at the beginning of the nineteenth century by a Briton named Lord Elgin. At that time, Greece was ruled by Turkey and many of the monuments had fallen into disrepair. However, it is uncertain whether Lord Elgin had permission to remove so many pieces. The sculptures were taken to London and a special room was built for them at the British Museum. Today, many people feel strongly that Athens is the proper home for the 'Elgin marbles'.

Athene Parthenos

In ancient times it was the statue of Athene Parthenos (Virgin Athene) which aroused most admiration. This statue was the work of Pheidias and was about 10 metres (33 feet) high.

The statue itself is made of ivory and gold. There is a sphinx on her helmet and carved griffins on either side. The statue of Athene is upright. Her chiton (dress) reaches to her feet and on her breast is the head of Medusa made of ivory. She is holding a statue of Victory, about 2 metres (6ft 6ins) high, and in her other hand is a spear. At her feet lies a shield, and near the shield is a serpent.   Pausanias 1.24.5

The fame of Pheidias' works made people jealous of him, especially because he included a likeness of himself on the shield of the goddess, fighting as a bald old man and lifting up a stone in battle against the

Shield dating from Roman times, thought to be a copy of the shield made by Pheidias for Athene's statue.

Statue of Athene discovered in a Roman house in Athens.

Amazons. He also included a very fine likeness of Pericles fighting one of the Amazons. The figure is holding a spear in front of his face as though Pheidias did not want the likeness to Pericles to be too obvious. Nevertheless, it is still quite clear if you look at it from either side.

Plutarch *Pericles* 21

Evidence for other monuments on the Acropolis

The Propylaea (gateway) and Temple of Athene Nike

There is only one possible way onto the Acropolis because the whole rock is so steep and has such a strong wall. The Propylaea has a roof of white marble and there is still nothing to match the beauty and size of its stones. On the right of the gateway is the temple of Athene Nike (Athene the Victor) and the sea is visible from this point. On the left of the gateway is a picture gallery.

Pausanias 1.22.4

The Erechtheum

The Erechtheum is named after Erechtheus, a legendary king of Athens.

Inside there is a well full of sea water. This is no great marvel, for other inland areas have them, but this one is remarkable because it makes the sound of waves when a south wind is blowing. On the rock is the outline of a trident. People say that these things appeared here as a sign of Poseidon's claim to the land. They have nothing to say about the olive tree, except that it was a sign of the goddess's claim to the land. They say that this olive was burned when the Persians set fire to the city, but that it grew again to the height of two cubits on the very same day.   Pausanias 1.26.4

The Erechtheum. In the foreground is the caryatid porch, in which the columns are replaced by female figures.

Statues

On the Athenian Acropolis there is also a statue of Pericles, the son of Xanthippus, and one of Xanthippus himself, who fought against the Persians in the sea battle of Mycale. The statue of Pericles stands separate from all the others.   Pausanias 1.25

There was another of Pheidias' famous works on the Acropolis: the statue of Athene Promachos (Athene the Warrior), dating from about 456 B.C.

The statue stood straight and was 30 feet high (nearly 9 metres). It was made of bronze and the clothing was also bronze. You could hardly take your eyes off her neck. It was long, and not concealed by the dress. As for the body, there was nothing stiff about it, the limbs were all as they should be, and you could see individual veins. There was a crest made of horsehair on her head.   Nicetas of Chonae
(writing in the thirteenth century A.D.)

Sailors can actually see the point of this Athene's spear and the crest of her helmet as they sail in from Cape Sounion.   Pausanias I.28.2

6 Two views of fifth-century Athens

Plato

Plato is thought to have written the *Gorgias* shortly after Socrates' death in 399 B.C. In this passage Socrates is comparing the care of the state with the nutrition of the body.

'You are full of praise for those men who have feasted the citizens on all the foods they wanted. People say that these men have made Athens great, but what they do not see is that the city is bloated and that this glow of health is only skin-deep – all because of those men in the olden days. They had no regard for moderation or what was right; instead, they stuffed the city full of harbours and dockyards and city walls and tribute – like so much junk food. Then, whenever the city's health goes into decline, everyone will hold responsible the people who are advising them at the time – and still sing the praises of Themistocles and Cimon and Pericles, the very men who caused the disease in the first place.'   Plato *Gorgias* 518D–519A

Thucydides

Pericles was chosen to give the speech at the funeral of those who had died in the first year of the Peloponnesian War. The speech, as written by Thucydides, not only concentrates on the war and on those who died fighting; it also expresses a view of Athens' ideals, way of life and achievements, and the following extracts are from these sections of the speech.

'Our form of government is no copy of our neighbours' laws. Far from imitating others, we are an example to them. Our form of government is called a democracy, that is, power in the hands of the whole people, not just a select few. When there are disputes between individuals, everyone is equal before the law. In public affairs, people are given a position because they deserve it: they get the job because of their own talent, not just because it is their turn. No one is kept out of the limelight just because he is poor, if he can be of some use to the city.

We are tolerant in our personal relationships, and in public life we do not break the law, because it is the law that we fear.

No one has provided more leisure activities than we have, so that we can relax our minds. Throughout the year there are contests and religious festivals, and in our homes there is elegance all around us. Every day our pleasure in all these things keeps us in a cheerful frame of mind. Our city is large enough to be able to import any goods from the whole world, so that we enjoy the products of other countries just as much as our own.

And look how different we are from our enemies in our attitude towards national security. For example, we let people come and go in our city as they please. Have we ever driven out foreigners for fear of their being spies and passing secrets to the enemy? No. We rely not on planning ahead or misleading our enemies, but on the courage we find within ourselves to face each action. We bring up our sons differently too: from childhood our enemies acquire bravery through hard training; we, on the other hand, live at ease and yet go out to meet dangers that are just as great. And where is the proof of this? Here, in our own land! The Spartans cannot invade on their own; they have to be backed up by all their allies! And ourselves? Why, we attack our neighbours' land and usually win, even though they are fighting on their home ground and we're on foreign ground.

We love beautiful things but are not extravagant; we love to exercise our minds but that does not make our bodies weak. We regard wealth as something that enables us to take action, not as something to boast about. No one should be ashamed to admit that he is poor – as long as he tries to escape from it. Men here are just as interested in the affairs of state as they are in their own, however varied the occupations of different individuals. People in other cities might say that a man who does not involve himself in the state is just minding his own business; we are the only people to say that a man like this has no use at all.

Finally, I say that Greece can learn from all aspects of our city, and it seems to me that among us one and and the same man would be ready to play his part in a wider range of situations than anywhere else and at the same time preserve his individuality. If you think I am just saying this as a boast, then here is the proof that it is true. You only have to look at the actual strength of the city – strength we have acquired by doing things in the way that I have described.   Thucydides II. 37–41 (extracts)